BEGINNINGS

*"Delight yourself in the Lord and He will
give you the desires of your heart"*

Psalm 37: 4

Karen Buford

DESIRE OF THE HEART
BEGINNINGS

iUniverse books may be ordered through booksellers or by contacting:

iUniverse
1663 Liberty Drive
Bloomington, IN 47403
www.iuniverse.com
1-800-Authors (1-800-288-4677)

ISBN: 978-1-4917-5431-3 (sc)
ISBN: 978-1-4917-5433-7 (hc)
ISBN: 978-1-4917-5432-0 (e)

Library of Congress Control Number: 2014921037

Print information available on the last page.

iUniverse rev. date: 3/31/2016

Chapter One

Sierra's world was shaken.

The unforeseen encounter triggered her to question everything she accepted as truth. The instantaneous tremble in her hand, the sensation of her heart melting within her body, and the fact that she could hardly breathe at the mere sight of Grayson caused her to rethink the notion of love at first sight.

Frozen at the threshold of the back door to the little country church she had grown up in, Sierra's life flashed before her eyes. Could this also be the threshold of the next chapter in her life? Could this be the answer to the prayers she was beginning to think God chose to ignore?

The rusty chairs arranged in a semi-circle around the old wooden podium in the center of the fellowship hall sparked a memory of childhood, a time Sierra often wished she could return to, a time before insecurity and distrust had become a part of her very being.

'Sierra, I want you to meet Grayson Raines, our new Associate Pastor,' said her mother, who was standing with him on the other side of the outdated, green and mustard yellow colored countertop separating the church's tiny kitchen from the fellowship hall with an antique piano in the corner where it had sat for over one-hundred years.

As she attempted to respond, Sierra's heart pounded uncontrollably. She became light headed. She could barely grip the glass in her hand. 'My goodness, what is happening to me,' she thought to herself as she rushed outside to regain her composure. At that moment she was glad that she parked her new little grey car near the back entrance of the church. She stumbled over to her car, put her glass on the hood, and took a few deep breaths.

She wasn't sure why, but Sierra knew that her life would never be the same again. She could not think straight enough to remember Grayson's last name, but she felt with every inch of her being that he was the man she would marry.

'But God, I am so unworthy of such a gift,' she said to herself. The same insecurity that has caused her to doubt God on so many occasions before this one crept into her thoughts – but only for a second. She knew she had to go back through that fellowship hall door again. She knew he would be standing there - waiting.

'Lord, carry me and speak through me right now because I can't walk on my own, and I am speechless,' Sierra prayed as she walked toward the rusty door. As she reached out for the handle, the door opened from the other side. 'Are you alright?' exclaimed Grayson as he reached out and touched her shoulder. The moment his hand made contact, Sierra felt a shock, like an electrified chill. It started from the top of her head, shot through her entire body, and exited through her feet. She felt weak, as if she were going to faint.

'Here, let me help you,' Grayson uttered as he took the glass and papers out of Sierra's hands. He sat them down on the cracked kitchen counter and grabbed one of the chairs from the semi-circle for Sierra to sit down in.

'No, no really – I am fine,' exclaimed Sierra. 'I don't want to sit down. I just needed to get some air, that's all.' She hated being the center of attention, yet she loved it at the same time. The feelings she was experiencing were new and quite overwhelming. What about PJ? How could she have these feelings for a man she knew for only five minutes when she had tossed the idea of love back and forth for nearly two years over PJ?

It was as if there was some sort of invisible force drawing her to Grayson. 'Um, what did you say your last name was again?' Sierra said quietly while nervously attempting to make eye contact with Grayson. 'Raines,' he responded with a deep, strong, voice that resonated throughout Sierra's entire being. 'It's nice to meet you,' Sierra managed to voice as she made a visual scan of Grayson from bottom to top. His burgundy dress shoes were shined to perfection.

Tomorrow would make one week since her honorable discharge from the United States Air Force, so she noticed such things. His khaki dress pants were perfectly fitted to his masculine frame. 'He must work out a lot,' Sierra thought as she noticed the tight, jutting muscles of his thighs beneath the fabric of his slacks. Moving her focus to his beltline, Sierra realized Grayson's waist was equally as tight, and his abs defined beneath his white dress shirt that was tucked neatly into his slacks and held in place with a gold buckled belt that matched his shoes. An emerald green, paisley tie hung from his neck between his broad shoulders and lay against his *man-of-steel* chest. Breathless, Sierra moved her glance upward to Grayson's face. As she quickly beheld his thin lips, his prominent nose, and clean-shaven jawline, her gaze became more focused. She fixed her interest on his crystal blue, hypnotizing eyes. Was it her imagination, or did Grayson feel the same mesmerizing chill upon his glance into her eyes? Just as she pulled away from the magnetized stare to notice his curly, dark hair, someone walked around the corner of the room by the old piano.

'Sierra will be bringing our special music in this morning's service,' Pastor Will Allen bellowed upon entering the fellowship hall on his way to the sanctuary and pulling on his suit coat. 'I see the two of you have already met. That relieves me of the responsibility of introducing you.' 'Finish up your planning, the service will begin in about ten minutes,' Pastor Allen said cheerfully as he rushed out the rusty door.

With a chuckle, Grayson broke the ice. 'Are you ready to sing? What song have you chosen? Let's look at the plans we have made for the service and see where it would best fit,' he suggested as he snapped back into reality. *Flowing Creek* was a traditional church.

Services were still conducted much the same way they had been at the time of the church's foundation.

Hymn number 78, *Rescue the Perishing*, was first on the agenda, followed by the opening prayer that would be brought by Brother Bill Younger. Greetings and welcome handshakes would be orchestrated by the instrumentalist's version of *We are One in the Bond of Love*. Tithes and offerings would follow as the ushers made their way to the front at the end of the instrumental ensemble. Prayer would then precede two more hymns to be chosen by the congregation. The choir members would then take their seats, and Sierra would be introduced by Pastor Allen as the one bringing special music before the message was delivered.

'Sounds like a plan to me,' responded Sierra as Grayson looked to her for approval. Gathering his papers, Grayson made a suggestion. 'Okay then, that's a plan, let me grab my sports coat and I will walk you to the sanctuary. Come this way, we will go in through the back entrance.'

'I am so nervous,' exclaimed Sierra. She wasn't sure if she was more nervous about singing in front of the whole congregation for the first time in years, or by the chance encounter that had rocked her entire world in the past thirty minutes, but her body trembled with a healthy fear that she had never experienced before that day. 'Sure, that's fine, you lead the way,' she said while she thought to herself, 'will he be the one to lead the way for the rest of my life?'

Because Grayson and Sierra were both on the agenda for the morning service, Pastor Allen directed them to the front pew where they were to sit as not to be a disturbance while making their way to the platform at the appropriate times. Sierra felt anxiously awkward, yet excited. She watched as Grayson got up and went forward to help Pastor Allen with a microphone cord that had become tangled under the platform. She had taken a good look at his features from the front in the fellowship hall, but now his back side was on display, and it was a pretty picture. When he leaned down to loosen the cord, his sports coat tightened up around his upper body. Sierra's heart again began pounding out of control. This guy was like a dream. Sierra didn't think there was actually a man who looked like him, much less one that she could aspire to spend her life with. Was she crazy? What was she thinking? Grayson was the kind of guy who would go for Miss America, and have no trouble getting her. How could she even think she had a chance with him? Those insecurities once again began to flood her mind.

Grayson stepped away from the platform, and returned to his seat. When he did, he patted Sierra on the knee and said to her, 'Don't be nervous, you are going to do a great job.' Sierra laughed inside at the realization that he had perceived her overwhelmed response to his display of manliness while loosening the cord to be her nerves acting up over the song she was to sing. Nevertheless, she was encouraged by his tender words.

Pastor Allen pulled on the microphone cord as he moved across the platform, introducing Grayson to the congregation saying, 'Brother Raines will now come and lead us in our opening hymn, followed by prayer by Brother Bill Younger... Brother Raines.' At his prompting, Grayson stood and made his way to the pulpit and opened his hymnal. 'Let's stand together and sing hymn number 78, *Rescue the Perishing.*' At that, the instrumentalist began to play. Judith Bradley, Sierra's mother, was the organist. She looked out into the congregation, made eye contact with Sierra, and winked her eye as if to say, 'I told you so.'

See, Judith's hunch was the reason Sierra was on the agenda to sing for the morning service in the first place. Two days before her discharge from the United States Air Force, Judith called Sierra on the phone. She told her that the congregation of *Flowing Creek Church* had recently hired a new Associate Pastor, she could not remember his name, but she thought it was Chase Rainey or something like that. She explained that the moment she saw him, she thought of Sierra. 'You have got to meet this guy when you come home, and when you do you are either going to love him or hate him.' Judith went on to explain that he was just one of those people with unique features that would either attract a person, or push them away. Obviously he wasn't pushing Sierra away, so her mother must have been right! 'Well Mother, I can't just walk in the church with you and say to him, 'Hi, my name is Sierra, my mom wanted me to meet you.' What can we do to make it not so obvious?' She wondered.

Never in a million years would Sierra have dreamed that her mother would call to set her up with a guy, especially one who was older than she was. Grayson was in his mid-to-late-twenties, just out of college, and a new Seminary Student in New Orleans. Sierra was almost twenty-two, just out of the service, and had yet to begin her college education. At the end of that initial phone call, once Sierra had agreed to meet the nameless man her mother spoke of, Judith said, 'You just come prepared to sing, I will take care of the rest.'

Sierra had sung in a Christian ensemble and in a Youth Choir while she was in high school, before she joined the service, but it had been years since she performed in public. She felt inadequate to say the least. Breathless and feeling unworthy, Sierra agreed to find a song and get prepared to sing in church when she returned to Louisiana. She hung up the phone; however, feeling a bit hypocritical. Since her days of singing in choirs and Christian ensembles, she had not exactly been a model Christian. Though she would be considered a 'good girl' in the eyes of most, she knew where she was, and felt ashamed and inadequate.

Parties, friends, and peer pressure had taken over where church events and devotion to the Lord had once dominated. Though there were lines she determined not to cross, her testimony was still not one that deemed her worthy of standing before a congregation to minister in any way, or so she felt. Anyway, how was she going to meet a guy who had been called into the ministry and was attending seminary without a drastic change in her own life? 'I will just give it a try,' she thought it could not hurt anything to make her mom happy.

Judith's wink sparked a timid smile in Sierra. She nodded her head in agreement, and felt a peace about the whole ordeal. 'Let us pray,' declared Brother Bill Younger. Sierra felt that she must have been day-dreaming through the whole first song, as she barely remembered anything past the opening notes. 'Pull your stuff together girl,' she secretly thought as Brother Bill prayed. 'Amen…now if you will shake hands with those around you while the instrumentalist play you will be blessed,' he said enthusiastically.

The people of the congregation seemed to make a bee-line to the front of the church to welcome Sierra home. Everyone was overjoyed to see her. 'Are you going to sing for us today honey,' Mrs. Edith said. 'You haven't aged one day, you are still a baby,' exclaimed Mrs. Rosie. 'When do you have to go back?' asked Mr. Roberts, along with 'What do you plan to do now that you are home,' when she explained to him that she had finished her enlistment and would not be returning to active duty. It was nice to feel welcome.

It was encouraging to be home with those who accepted her unconditionally. Sierra still felt a bit like she was floating, but her nerves did begin to settle down some after such a warm reception. As the instrumentalist came to the end of the song, *We Are One in the Bond of Love*, the congregation was prompted to return to their seats. Only a few stragglers chose to give Sierra a belated welcome hug before they found their seats, but it was not too distracting.

'I would like to ask our ushers to come forward at this time to take up the morning offering,' Pastor Allen charged the men. Four men dressed in their Sunday best came to the front and stood around the table. Brother Andrew Cox said, 'let's pray for the gifts we are about to receive.' With that, the men systematically walked down the aisles, passing the offering plates from person to person.

Sierra realized that she was next on the agenda. She became nervous, this time actually about the singing. She took a deep breath, sipped a drink of water from the glass she had focused on not spilling since she sat down in the pew, and asked the Lord to take over where she felt inadequate. Before she knew it, Grayson rose from his seat and walked toward the microphone.

'We are blessed today to have with us a guest who is no stranger to *Flowing Creek Church*, Miss Sierra Bradley, she has recently returned home from the Air Force, and is going to bring our special music this morning. So, Sierra, why don't you come on up and bless us today.' 'Whew! This is it,' she thought as she stood and made her way toward Grayson. When she stepped upon the platform, he reached over and gave her a hug and whispered in her ear, 'I will be praying for you the whole time, you will do great!' Sierra was overwhelmed and encouraged as she stood before the people who loved and missed her, and she began to speak.

'Um, I feel a bit inadequate standing here before you this morning. It amazes me how an almighty God can look beyond our faults, and love us unconditionally. I feel unworthy to be used by the Lord, but in obedience, I bring this message to you in song. As I do, please listen; not to me, but to the words that I sing, because that is why God wanted me to be here today,' Sierra thought to herself with those last words, 'at least I thought that was why God wanted me to be here today – boy was I mistaken!' She gave the sound man a thumb's up. As the music began, she looked out in the crowd and saw Grayson. He was smiling a pleasant smile and giving her a thumbs-up of his own, and said, 'Just let go.'

Sierra sang the song, *"Holy Lord,"* like she never had before. It was as if the people in the room disappeared, and she stood face-to-face with the Lord as she sang. Such a healing and a cleansing took place in her personal life during those three minutes that it seemed like hours. The fact that there is no condemnation for those who seek the Lord resonated within her spirit. She hit the final note of the song a different person than she had hit the first. This had been a day like no other, and it was only eleven o'clock in the morning.

Chapter Two

Sierra sat thoughtfully throughout the remainder of the morning service, hauntingly aware of her every move. Thoughts like how she was holding her hands, where her eyes were fixed, whether she crossed her legs or not, and more than anything else, whether or not her stomach would growl loud enough for Grayson to hear it, occupied her thoughts and distracted her from comprehending a single word of the Pastor's sermon.

About half-way through the message, Grayson leaned forward to take off his sports coat. Sierra noticed that he was struggling to get his arm out of the sleeve while sitting down. She reached over to clutch the bottom of it when her freshly manicured fingernails brushed unexpectedly against the palm of his calloused hand. Anxious by the touch, Sierra whispered as she drew her hand back, 'Would you like me to help you?' 'Ye -yes, thank you! That would be great,' he replied with a magnificent smile.

As the sleeve was pulled off, Sierra could not help but notice the well-developed form of Grayson's arms. 'What in the world does this guy do,' she thought. He looked like a cover model for *You Name It* Magazine. Grayson folded the coat in half and handed it to Sierra as he asked her to lay it over the pew beside her.

When Sierra took the coat, her senses were awakened by the sweet smelling cologne that embraced the very fabric of the garment. She closed her eyes and took a deep breath, hoping he would not notice the delay in her doing what he had asked of her - because that would just be uncanny. For the remainder of the service, all Sierra could think about was the scent of Grayson's cologne.

When the service ended, Sierra did not want to seem over-zealous. She hastily told Grayson it was nice to meet him and that she hoped to see him again, then she decidedly walked away to chat with others who had missed the opportunity to welcome her home during the greeting time at the beginning of the service. Certainly, that was not what she wanted to do. She wanted to stand right where she was and watch Grayson, waiting for him to ask her out to dinner or for her phone number, or just anything - but she resisted.

Judith yelled across the room, 'Sierra, I am going to go on home, I will meet you there!' 'I am right behind you mom,' Sierra replied. Grayson heard the exchange of words and spoke a soft, 'I was really nice to meet you,' his blue eyes fixed intently on her with a penetrating gaze.

Laura Trahan stood in the back of the church with her arms crossed, tapping her half painted fingertips against the Bible in her right hand. Her bewildered look puzzled Sierra, but she didn't allow it to bother her. She had known Laura since they were in pre-school. She was always perturbed by something Sierra was doing, so why should this day be any different? A fiery red-head, Laura was always tempered when things were not going her way.

When she got to her car, Sierra realized that she had forgotten her keys in the fellowship hall where Grayson had laid them on the counter-top after her initial, feeble entrance. She dropped her purse and things off in the back seat of her car then headed to that same old rusty door to find her keys.

As if it were a replay of the morning episode, Sierra arrived at the door just as it swung open with Grayson standing on the other side. 'Well... long time no see,' he laughed upon almost literally running into Sierra again. He was headed to the church van to bring some of the youth home from the service.

'Oh, I think I left my keys in the fellowship hall and I was coming to get them,' Sierra managed to utter, though her heart felt like it was going to burst at one more pleasant yet unforeseen encounter. Grayson held the door with his perfectly shined shoe as he leaned over and picked Sierra's keys up off of the countertop where he had laid them earlier. Placing them in Sierra's palm, Grayson used his free hand to cradle the bottom of her hand. He gripped tightly enough that Sierra could not pull away, not that she wanted to, but gently enough that she felt the same deep compassion and tenderness from his hands that she witnessed in his gorgeous blue eyes. She hated to walk away. She was under his spell.

Grayson eventually released her hand, gave her a wink, and walked toward the van. It was obvious that the teenagers who waited for their ride home were aware that something more than a simple goodbye had just taken place before their eyes. Sierra turned and walked to her car, this time she actually sat down and started the engine.

Before she drove away, Sierra rested her head against the back of her seat and reflected upon the previous two hours of her life. They undoubtedly left an impression – one she was certain would never fade away.

'Grayson Raines - why you, why today, and what would this turn out to be?' A flood of emotion came over her. 'There must be something to this. God must have a plan, but it could not have happened at a more inconvenient time,' she felt.

'What will I tell PJ,' she thought as she finally put the car in drive. Patrick Jennings, aka PJ had been her steady for nearly two years. He would always shrink from the idea of a bona fide commitment, especially marriage. Sierra didn't push him. She knew he was not a Christian.

Her mother's words echoed in her mind a million times, 'Do not be yoked together with a nonbeliever.' But - Sierra was sure she loved PJ. She had often dreamt of spending the rest of her life with him. He, on the other hand was not willing to discuss such things. He lived for the moment. Life was supposed to be fun, commitment was not fun. She assumed his goal was to elude responsibility for as long as he possibly could.

'I will just cross that bridge when I come to it. PJ is on a training mission for the next week anyway,' with that thought her confidence grew stronger. PJ was an Army Ranger in training for the 82nd Air Borne Battalion. His primary focus was to advance in his Army career, and he was doing a fine job of that. He was from Malibu Beach, California. That was the most intriguing aspect, at least to uncultured Sierra.

Sierra had spent her entire life in *La Maison*, Louisiana. She was definitely not cultured. PJ; on the other hand was. He was twenty-four, and his black military style haircut caused his black eyes to pop. He was a surfer, how cool is that! And, he drove around the base on a fast, blue and white street bike. He wore white leathers, and even got a set of leathers for Sierra so that she could ride with him in style. Money was not an issue for PJ; his dad was the CEO of some big company in San Francisco, even more fascinating!

Everyone knew that PJ and Sierra together were like a 'wink and a smile.' He loved to hear her talk. Her southern accent hooked him and kept him hooked for two years, whether he admitted it or not. He was also gripped by her tiny frame. Sierra was only five feet tall and weighed all of 115 pounds. She was like a little doll; at least that is what PJ always told her.

Today; however, for the first time in two years, Sierra felt relieved that PJ had never asked her to marry him. She was young and zealous. If PJ had proposed; she would have gone to the moon to marry him without even considering the consequences. She was immature, and infatuated, not in love. She realized that now. The shadow of doubt that had hovered over her for two years had instantly transformed into calm assurance. PJ was not the one. She was over him. Only God could have given that assurance.

Sierra's parents lived only about three miles from *Flowing Creek Church*, so the trip home was not a long one. As she pulled her little car into the driveway, Sierra noticed others had arrived before her.

Two of her three brothers were waiting for her to get home. They had been working, and this was their first chance to see her since she got back to Louisiana. Before she could get the car parked, her brother Josh and his wife Andrea stepped out of the front door waving and smiling. 'It is so great to see you! You look beautiful,' exclaimed Andrea as soon as Sierra stepped out of the car. She was glad to hear those encouraging words, 'Maybe if Andrea thinks I look beautiful, Grayson did too,' she thought.

'You cut your hair,' she heard Alisa, her other sister-in-law, shout from the backyard. Sierra had always had long, brown hair. It was a trademark of sorts of her. Having to put it up every day that she was in uniform got laborious, and PJ suggested she get it cut. 'Why not,' she thought. Then; about six months ago, she jumped on the back of PJ's motorcycle and had him take her to the beauty shop. He helped her pick out a style that he thought would suit her, and that was all she wrote. She liked it, it made her look older, or at least she thought it did. PJ said it was cute, which made her second guess herself. She didn't want to look cute - she wanted to look beautiful, or at least pretty. A cute baby doll, uuugghh!!

At that moment Judith chimed in, 'Well I don't care what anyone else thinks, I love it short and I think you should keep it that way.' Sierra was still unsure about the style being permanent; but she was sure glad everyone liked it.

As Sierra reached into her back seat to gather her things, her oldest brother, Grant rounded the corner with Stan, her dad. Grant was not the most affectionate one of the family; he was a lot like his dad. The words *I Love You* were hard to come by, but the notion was definitely implied. Sierra knew they loved her and were glad to see her home. Her dad can't give her a hug without lifting her up off of the ground and popping her back. She knew what she was in for as soon as she saw him coming her way. First, Grant reached out to empty her hands and said, 'Here, I will take that,' it was his way of avoiding the affectionate stuff, at least that is what Sierra thought. Her hands were free, so of course, the back popping hug was next on the agenda. Stan said, 'Come here girl,' and then lifted her off the ground, shaking her little body with one jolt, causing every vertebrate in her back to snap simultaneously. 'Ok daddy, it won't pop anymore. You can put me down,' exclaimed Sierra with a lighthearted tone.

With that, everyone headed into the house. 'Boy it sure smells good in here,' Sierra voiced as she walked through the front door. 'What's for lunch?' 'Your favorite, Shrimp Etouffette,' Judith answered in a loving manner. It was the fresh French bread in the oven that had tantalized her senses, however.

'Let me change into something more comfortable and I will help you set the table,' Sierra told her mother as she headed to the bedroom. Sierra closed the bedroom door behind her and fell backwards onto the bed just as she used to do in the swimming pool when she was a kid. Her arms out to her side like she was free as a bird, she landed on the mattress and bounced a time or two before the pillow-top softness engulfed her tiny frame.

All she could think about was Grayson...and PJ, but mostly Grayson. The image of his tight thighs, his massive arms, and his superman-like torso engulfed her mind. Those eyes, there was something magical in his stunning blue eyes that captured her from the depths of her being. 'Mrs. Sierra Raines, how would that sound,' she thought. 'Sierra Nicole Raines has a nice ring to it, better than Sierra Nicole Jennings, I like it,' she thought. Then she snapped to reality and jumped off of the bed.

'Whew, let me pick out something to wear and get in there where they need my help before I fall asleep,' she whispered aloud to herself as she slid out of the little black dress she had worn to church.

Slipping into a purple and gold LSU sweat suit, and pulling her hair; that was just now long enough to fit into a tiny ponytail back, she skipped toward the kitchen like she was fifteen again.

She said, 'What can I do?' She wanted to be a part of the family environment again, it had been so long. She was taking it all in.

'Sierra, you can put ice in the glasses and find out what everyone wants to drink. We have just about anything you can imagine,' Judith instructed. Sierra did just that. 'Two cokes, one diet, and the rest sweet tea. Two cokes, one diet, and the rest sweet tea,' she rehearsed after getting everyone's request so that she would not forget.

When the drinks were ready, she carried them to the table two at a time. Andrea was three months pregnant. When Josh saw that she had coke in her glass, he politely rebuked her saying, 'Andrea, you know the baby doesn't need that. You need to drink water.' Andrea looked at Josh nearly teary-eyed and said, 'Just this once Josh, I am sick and tired of drinking water, if you were the one carrying this baby maybe you would understand.'

A blanket of silence fell over the room as everyone waited for Josh's response. Everyone knew that his reply would either make the situation worse or make it better. Trying to make facial expressions to direct Josh's response, Judith cleared her throat in an effort to gain his attention.

'Ok baby, you know what you need, but I wouldn't make it a habit,' replied Josh. Everyone let out a sigh of relief and began fixing their plates. Andrea smiled. About the time Sierra was going to sit down to fix her plate, the phone rang. 'I'll get it she said, since I am the only one still up.'

She thought surely it would be Travis, her twin brother calling from New Mexico where he was still stationed. He too had joined the Air Force directly out of high school, but planned to make a career of it.

'Hello, this is Sierra speaking,' she said as she put the phone to her ear. Her knees buckled when she heard PJ on the other end of the line.

'I miss you baby, when can I come see you?'

'Oh...PJ, I wasn't expecting to hear your voice, I thought you were in training this week.'

'I am, but I asked for a little break so that I could hear your voice. I don't know, but ever since you left, all I can think about is you.' As he spoke those words Sierra slid to the floor in the corner of her mom's kitchen, lifeless and speechless at the same time. She nearly dropped the phone.

He continued, 'I don't know how I am going to live without you here, everything seems so empty with you gone. I don't have a motivation to get up in the morning, to get off of work in the evenings, or to look forward to the weekend.'

'PJ, why are you doing this to me now? I thought you were not ready for a commitment. That was the last thing we talked about before I left?' she replied.

'I thought so too, but since you have been gone I have had time to truly reflect on my life. I realize something that I had never realized before now.' 'What's that,' Sierra said nervously.

'I – I think I love you Sierra.'

Sierra didn't know how to respond. 'Um…PJ, I have to talk to you about something, but now is not a good time. Can you call me back later when everyone is not listening?'

'I will try, if possible tonight. Can you be around the phone at eleven-thirty your time? That is probably the only time I can get away to call again.' 'Yes, I should be here, I have church tonight, but it will be over by then,' Sierra responded. 'I look forward to it,' she said out of habit and in an effort to avoid responding with 'I love you too.'

The last words she heard before hanging up the phone and breathing a deep sigh were, 'Bye angel.' As Sierra picked her limp body up off of the floor and tried to regain her composure, her mother walked in and said, 'Is everything alright?' Feeling numb, Sierra thought about lying and saying that everything was just fine. But she decided it was time to be honest, 'No, I am in a total whirlwind and I don't know what I am going to do about it,' she said to Judith as she headed back to her seat and plopped down like a rag-doll.

'Okay, so let's talk about it,' Alisa said emphatically. 'We are your family, that's why we are here. What happened,' prompted Alisa.

'You are going to think I am crazy, but I am just going to say it like it is,' Sierra began to explain. 'I have been dating PJ for almost two years, I know you know that, but you have not had the privilege of meeting him because he was afraid of the whole, 'meet the family thing' and he was not ready for a commitment. So, that was him on the phone. He got permission to take a break from his rigorous training schedule, which is unheard of, to call me and tell me that he doesn't know how he is going to live without me. He has had time to evaluate our relationship, and his life, and he realized that he finally thinks he loves me and he wants to come down here to see me and meet the family.'

'That's fantastic Sierra! Congratulations!' shouted Andrea. Sierra sighed. Josh kicked Andrea underneath the table. 'What's wrong honey, aren't you excited?' Andrea responded to her reaction. Sierra pushed her plate away, leaned forward resting her elbows on the table, and covered her eyes with her hands in dismay. 'This is what I have been waiting for! This is what I wanted for so long, but today of all days, something happened that changed my thoughts, changed my feelings, and changed my mind about PJ altogether,' Sierra cried.

'What is it Sierra, what happened,' demanded her dad. 'It...it was Grayson, I don't know how–but when I saw him this morning something happened inside of me. As crazy as it sounds, it is like I know he is the one I am supposed to marry. I don't even know him, so I must be losing my mind. And now, I come home all confused about my chance encounter with Grayson and PJ calls to say he can't live without me and he thinks he loves me. I don't know what to do!' 'How can I be feeling this way about a guy I just met? How can the past two years of my life with PJ end just like that? Am I crazy?'

Chapter Three

'Oh honey, let me tell you something that I learned years ago,' her mother chimed in. 'It doesn't matter how much you think you love PJ, if you can have feelings for another man you can be sure that he is not the one you are supposed to marry. When God puts the right one in your life, you will never, ever have a desire or even a pull towards another man.'

'She is right,' replied Josh, 'Even I can vouch for that. When I was dating, I always got tired of the relationships after a few months and began looking for something more, or something better in another, but when I met Andrea, that changed. I can honestly tell you that the empty place in my heart that I had been trying to fill was intended for her all along. It is almost like God made her just for me. I am complete, I have no need and no desire for anything more. That is how you know it is a God thing.' Andrea blushed with those words, and smiled at Josh.

'Well, I have been waiting for PJ to show some interest in God. He always says that he is not religious. I tried to tell him over and over again that it was not about being religious, it was about accepting Jesus in his heart, but he was never ready to do that. That was the main reason that I felt he may not be the one for me, but I always held out hope that he would become a Christian and change his life. I really didn't think I could have feelings for another man. But this morning blew that idea right out of the water. My world has been rocked, and Grayson doesn't even know it!' Sierra laughed.

'So, PJ is going to call me back tonight at eleven-thirty tonight. Should I just tell him it's over since I have feelings for another man?' Sierra asked with anticipation. 'I feel crazy even saying that since Grayson may never even talk to me again. What if this morning was just a passing obsession that threw my head in the clouds, what if I am imagining things?' Stan put in his two cents, 'Honesty is the best policy, it is going to be hard for him to understand how you can be home for only a week and have feelings for another man already, but you have to tell PJ that it is a God thing.' 'Whether or not anything comes out of your encounter with Grayson this morning, you know that your heart is not completely filled by the relationship with PJ. That is enough for you to understand that no matter what God's plan is for you and Grayson, the future is not planned out for you to be with PJ. God is telling you to move on,' he insisted.

Sierra's head felt like it was spinning, she could not even begin to eat her lunch. 'Ok, I know you guys are right, I just have to try to stop thinking about it. Go ahead and eat, I am just going to go lay down for a little while, if that's alright, all of this has worn me out. I feel weak.' 'Okay honey, don't worry about us, we will get the kitchen cleaned up, you just rest for a while,' Judith said with an encouraging tone.

Grant interjected, 'But when you wake up, we want to hear all about military life.' 'Sure thing Grant, that's a promise,' Sierra said as she headed to the back bedroom where she could already feel the pillow-top mattress against her back.

Refusing to think, Sierra forced herself to curl up under the covers and close her eyes. It didn't take long before she was sound asleep.

'I never felt good about that PJ guy anyway,' Stan grumbled as he buttered his French bread. 'Anyone too good to meet our family is not good enough for Sierra anyway,' he continued.

'I am just thankful God is directing her away from him, I was afraid she would end up marrying him and moving to Timbuktu. Then we would never see her again,' Judith confessed.

'So; Andrea, how have you been feeling lately?' Alisa said in an effort to change the subject. 'I feel good; I am just tired a lot. I have not really been sick, so that is a good thing, Andrea proudly announced. She had about another month before she could find out if the baby was a boy or a girl. She and Josh are keeping the names they have chosen a secret, and it is driving Stan crazy. 'Well, if it's a boy you should call him Eli, that's a good strong name,' he insisted. 'And if it's a girl, call her Emma. I had a mule named Emmer when I was a boy, and it was the best worker on our whole farm. Emma is a good female name, and maybe she would be a hard worker like Emmer if you gave her that name,' Stan was really good at giving his opinion. Josh and Andrea just laughed, 'We will keep those names in mind Mr. Stan,' Andrea respectfully replied, knowing that neither would be their choice.

'The food was great mom,' Grant complimented as he carried his plate to the sink. 'Go on in there and watch the football game Grant, I will help your mom clean the kitchen,' Alisa insisted. 'Andrea, you sit down and talk to us while we get things cleaned up, you don't need to be on your feet,' Judith demanded. 'No, I will not sit down yet, the least I can do is clean off the table,' Andrea averred. 'Okay then, the table... then you have a seat, and that's an order,' Judith exacted. Everyone laughed.

Judith and Stan's doorbell had a catchy little ring to it. When Sierra and Travis were young, they would often ring it just to hear the tune, and to drive everyone else in the house nuts, ding, ding, ding, ding, bong, bong, bong, bong. Sometimes Sierra could hear that sound in her sleep. As she rolled over on the pillow-top mattress, she wondered if she was dreaming again, or if she had just heard that doorbell. As she sat up in an effort to acclimate herself to her environment, and to wake up, she heard it again, ding, ding, ding, ding, bong, bong, bong, bong. This time she knew it was not a dream. Someone was there. She jumped up, and ran to the bathroom to fix up her ponytail that had all but slipped out, thinking that someone was dropping by to welcome her home. She brushed her teeth to be on the safe side.

She thought, 'How long have I been asleep?' As she drug her feet down the hallway toward the living room, she could hear Josh and Stan yelling, 'Go, Go, Go, – at the television.' Their team was about to make a touchdown. Grant was intently watching as well, but holding his breath rather than yelling. The game was just about over, this touchdown would determine the winner of the game. With that thought, Sierra realized that she had been asleep for at least three hours.

'We knew you must really be tired, so we didn't want to bother you. Did you sleep well,' Andrea asked. 'Apparently I did, I only meant to lie down for a few minutes, someone should have gotten me up,' Sierra said with a little embarrassment in her voice. 'No, you needed the rest, and we aren't doing anything but sitting around listening to the guys act like idiots over a football game, so you are fine, Alisa retorted.

'Who's that at the door,' yelled Stan. 'It's Pastor Allen,' answered Judith. 'He wanted to make sure we would be at church tonight,' she said.

'Yes Pastor Allen, we will be there, and we will be sure to have Sierra with us when we come, thank you for taking the time to stop by,' Sierra overheard her mother saying at the front door.

'You will make sure you have me with you when you do what,' Sierra called out to her mom. 'Oh, um – Pastor Allen was just coming by to see if you were going to be at church tonight. Apparently over their lunch, Grayson Raines mentioned that he hoped you would be back, so Pastor Allen thought he would drop by to make sure you were invited.'

'I see, so now he too is playing match-maker,' Sierra smirked. She was anxiously excited about the thought of seeing Grayson again, but even more taken aback that he had actually mentioned her name over lunch, and hoped to see her again that night.

'Oh, what will I wear,' Sierra's mind began to whirl. What time was it, how much time did she have to get ready? She ran nervously around the kitchen trying to hide her excitement. It didn't work. Andrea noticed immediately. 'Sierra, come over here and sit down, you need to get something to eat, you didn't even have lunch and it is already four-thirty. 'Oh, I don't think I can eat, I can't even breathe,' Sierra responded without a pause. She was truly being swept off of her feet. She could barely think straight, but one thing was for sure, it was not PJ who was causing her to float around like she was in a cloud.

'Okay, okay, I will get something to eat since I have time before church,' Sierra agreed. 'Oh, one more thing,' Judith said as she stepped back and poked her head around the corner before joining Stan for the end of the game, 'Grayson said that if you were going to be at church tonight, he would like for you to come in a talk to the youth about what it was like being in the Air Force. The youth meet separate from the adults on Sunday nights.'

'Oh my goodness, this is really happening isn't it,' Sierra said as she fixed herself a hearty helping of Shrimp Etouffette. Alisa and Andrea gave each other confirming glances across the kitchen table behind Sierra's back. They knew that something was happening that was out of Sierra's control. They were anxiously excited as well. 'I think maybe I will go to church tonight too,' Alisa declared. 'Do you want to come with me,' she said to Andrea. 'Yes, I think that would be great, I just need to get ready,' Andrea replied.

Sierra turned around with a convinced grin on her face, 'you guys don't fool me. You just want to be nosey.' 'No, it is not just that. We want to see what this guy looks like. Our family is filled with beautiful people, we have to make sure we approve of whoever it is you may be pulling into it,' Andrea said jokingly. 'Goodness guys, I barely know his name, and you are already going for an approval visit,' Sierra snapped with a shy smile on her face. 'Yes, we are, now go ahead and eat before you blow away,' Alisa demanded.

Sierra could not remember how long it had been since she had eaten Shrimp Etouffette, and no one could fix it like her mother could. Every bite was like heaven in her mouth. She was so happy to be home, and so encouraged by the family God had given her. Her focus had been distorted for so long. Whatever it was that had happened to her when she was singing this morning was real. She knew that now without a doubt. The whole world seemed brighter. The future had purpose, and the prayers Sierra had prayed for years all seemed like they were being answered at the same time. Amazingly, her desires were not even the same. What she had tossed around in her mind for years had diminished without any effort on her part, suddenly her only desire was of the heart. She didn't even understand what that meant.

'What time does church start tonight mom?' Sierra asked. 'It starts at 6:00 p.m. honey, so you had better go ahead and get ready, you don't want to be late,' Judith answered. Normally Sierra would not bother to take another shower, but she wanted to start over and be fresh tonight. She carried her plate to the sink, thanked her mother, told Andrea and Alisa she needed to hurry up and get ready, then she rushed off to the back bathroom. As she stepped into the shower, Sierra went through her mind thinking of every piece of clothing in her still unpacked suitcase. 'What should I wear, what should I wear, I need to look neat, but modest at the same time, she thought.'

She knew *Flowing Creek Church* well, so as far as everyone else in the congregation was concerned, she could have gone just exactly as she was in the LSU sweats with her hair pulled back, but she wanted to make a better impression than that on this Grayson who inquired about her attendance.

'I will fix my hair and make-up first,' she thought to herself as she stepped out of the shower and rubbed her arms with the perfumed lotion that came with the bottle of cologne her mother had given her as a gift upon her return. *Gorgeous*, how appropriate, that is just the way she wanted to feel and look. Though she didn't feel like she was really gorgeous, Sierra hoped Grayson would.

Her hair had grown long enough to fit hot rollers around it. So she decided that was what she would do to fix it for church. Once the rollers were in, she applied her make-up. Once that was done, and before she stepped out of the bathroom to pick out an outfit, she went ahead and took the rollers down from her hair. She ran her fingers through each curl, shook her head, and looked in the mirror, 'Thank you, Lord! It looks exactly like I had hoped it would, now please just let it stay like this tonight,' she prayed out loud.

'What about those black pants, I could wear them with the orange top,' she thought. 'No, that would look too much like Halloween. I could wear the pink top, but maybe that looks too much like a kid.' As she dug to the bottom of her suitcase, Sierra remembered the brown pants and thin, tan, sweater that was in the trunk of her car. She had put them there on her way home so that if she decided to change before she got to her parent's house she would not have to dig in the luggage. 'Yes, that is it. I will go get that outfit. Thank you God!!'

Sierra got the outfit, along with a pair of tan sandals out of her trunk, ran inside to put them on, and waited for Andrea. 'It is about ten till six,' Judith announced as she headed toward the door, 'Anyone riding with me needs to be in the car before I put it in reverse.' 'Go ahead mom,' Alisa called out, 'Andrea is almost ready, she and Sierra can ride with me.' 'Okay, but don't be late!' Judith said as she closed the door behind her.

'I'm ready mom,' Sierra shouted, 'Andrea; I will just ride with mom. I will see you there!" Sierra didn't want to take a chance on being late and having to interrupt the youth meeting when she arrived. She thought it would be best to go with her mother and get there on time.

Judith could see that Sierra was nervous with anticipation. 'You look really pretty, I think Grayson will be glad you came,' she said to her. 'Thanks mother, you always know what to say to make me feel better about things. You know you got me into this mess don't you,' Sierra cast the blame on her mother. 'No honey, this was not me, it was a God thing, and don't you forget it!' With that, Judith backed out of the driveway and headed to the church.

Chapter Four

As Sierra stepped out of her mother's car and headed toward the rusty door of the fellowship hall, she half expected it to open before she reached the handle. This time; however, that was not the case. She opened the door and walked in with no one to greet her on the other side. No one was there at all, at least not in the fellowship hall. She could hear laughter down the hallway, so she walked toward the sound. 'Maybe the youth don't meet in here on Sunday nights anymore,' she thought to herself as she went toward the voices down the hall. Her assumption was correct, the voices led her to a room that had been the nursery in the days that she attended *Flowing Creek Church*. It had been redecorated and turned into a youth room upon Grayson's arrival.

Comfortable, mismatched couches lined the walls. An enormous red and black rug was thrown in the center of the huge, square room with a wooden podium sitting on it. It looked as if everyone in the congregation had dropped off the furniture they no longer needed so the youth could use it to make their own little club. It appeared to work for them, about thirty teenagers were there. Some were wrestling around and having a great time on the rug, others were sitting on the couches cheering them on.

'Do you guys know if Grayson is here yet?' Sierra asked awkwardly. 'Yeahhhhh – are you his new girlfriend? He's a lucky dog,' yelled out one of the teenagers. Embarrassed and turning red in the face, Sierra said, 'No, I am not his girlfriend, I am here to speak to the youth tonight, can you tell me where I can find Grayson?' A tall, brutish looking guy who was obviously one of the older youth yelled out from the rug, 'Well, if you aren't his girlfriend, would you be mine?' 'Come on Guys, where can I find Grayson? I need to talk with him before we get started with the youth meeting tonight,' Sierra called their bluff. A couple of the girls got up from the couches and directed her to his office down the hall.

Sierra was nervous, but tried not to show it. One of the girls asked, 'Are you the one who sang this morning?' 'Actually, yes, I am. My name is Sierra, what's yours?' 'Mine is Amanda and hers is Kate, you have a really pretty voice. Are you going to sing again tonight?' She asked. 'No, I am only going to talk tonight, but thank you. That was really sweet.'

'Grayson's office is right here, he is usually in there until it is time for the meeting to start, we have about five minutes,' Kate said. 'Thanks girls, I really appreciate it. I will see you back in the youth room in a few minutes,' Sierra said before she knocked on the door. She smiled because she heard the girls chuckling as they ran back down the hall toward the youth room. They knew something was up.

With a knock at the door she heard Grayson stand up from his chair. 'Come in,' he said with his deep masculine voice. Sierra took one last, deep breath and opened the door. 'Come in – please, sit down, just keep the door opened if you don't mind, that's just a precaution I always take,' Grayson spouted nervously as Sierra walked into his office and grabbed a seat. 'So, are you ready to speak to the youth tonight? I really appreciate your willingness to come on such short notice,' Grayson said. It was obvious to Sierra that she was not the only one anxious and feeling awkward about this meeting. 'Well, Brother Allen said you would like me to tell the youth what life was like in the Air Force, so there was really nothing to prepare. I only have one story, I figured I would just tell it and answer any questions the kids might have. Does that sound like a plan?' She asked. "You and your plans, yes, it does. That sounds great, so if you are ready then I am ready. Let's go!' Grayson encouraged Sierra as he took off his windbreaker and placed it on the coat-rack in the corner of his tiny office.

He was no longer wearing a tie. He had changed into a navy-blue jogging suit. When he took off his windbreaker, the red t-shirt underneath was clinging to his ripped abs until he pulled on the bottom of it to straighten it out. It was only for a second, but long enough to remind Sierra that what she had seen earlier was not only a dream. It was standing before her in real life! Grayson winked at Sierra and said, 'Follow me.'

'I will follow you anywhere,' Sierra thought as she turned out the light and closed Grayson's office door. 'I will just sit down and let you do what you normally do, then when you are ready for me to speak you can let me know, okay,' Sierra said, obviously feeling inadequate. 'That sounds like a plan,' Grayson said sarcastically with a smirk on his face.

'I think he is flirting with me, I really hope he is flirting with me,' Sierra thought as she followed him to the youth room and took a seat in the corner on a fold-out chair rather than getting too comfortable with the kids on the couches.

'Okay guys, I have something special for you tonight,' Grayson said enthusiastically in an effort to gain their attention. 'I'll bet you do Gray-boy,' one of the teenage boys from across the room teased. 'Just how special is it Mr. Raines?' said another. It was apparent that Grayson was a bit uncomfortable with the accusations - as he became a bit fidgety. 'Now guys, that's enough. Tonight we are going to play a game, then we will have a special guest speak to us about what life is like in the United States Air Force. After that, if everyone gives her your undivided attention, you will find out what I have for you that is special. Does that sound like a plan?' With those words, Grayson glared over at Sierra and gave her a wink and a thumbs-up.

'Oh boy, he is flirting! I can't let him see that I am flustered. Sierra, just act normal, be calm, and don't do anything stupid,' she thought.

Grayson grabbed two huge trash-cans and placed them at the far end of the room. He moved the podium off of the rug, and told everyone to stay seated, and keep the middle of the floor unoccupied. He brought out a bag full of ping pong balls and some duck-tape. He walked to the end of the room opposite the trash-cans and placed a strip of tape about a foot long in two spots behind the rug.

Grayson explained, 'I will divide the group into two teams. Whichever team you are on will determine which tape line you should stand behind when your name is called. When it is your turn, stand behind the tape line. Your objective is to bounce the ping pong ball one time and make it into the trash-can on your side of the line. You may not throw the ping pong ball directly into the trash-can. You may not step across the tape line, and you may not make the ball into the trash-can of the other team. You must stand behind your team's tape line, bounce the ping pong ball in such a manner that it goes from the rug to the trash-can designated for your team. Each ball that makes it into the appropriate trash-can amounts to one point. The team with the most points after each team member has taken a turn wins. Does everyone understand?'

'Yes, we understand.' They answered in unison. With that, Grayson started down one side of the room and up the other, "1, 2, 1, 2, 1, 2, 1, 2… until everyone was given a number. 'Okay, all of the one's get on this side of the room and all of the twos get on that side of the room – Go!'

Sierra was amazed at how much control he had over the kids. He was really good with them. He knew what he wanted, and he knew how to make them comply. She liked that about him, if she were honest with herself, she would have to admit that she liked everything about him. More than that; however, Sierra enjoyed watching him run around the room, and she loved listening to his voice. 'I don't even know this guy, what is wrong with me!' She thought still wondering what he did to make himself look like a body builder.

'Now, before you get started, Sierra and I are going to demonstrate how this game works for you,' Grayson surprised Sierra with those words to say the least. 'Is he joking, I don't know how to play this game,' Sierra responded immediately. 'Exactly, that's why we need you to demonstrate. They don't know how to play either, so they can learn from your mistakes before they make their own.'

'This guy is a practical joker. He is playing games with me already, I am not sure how to take it. Alright, alright, I will give it a shot, but I am not much of a game player, so don't take any pointers from me. 'Woo-hoo!' the kids yelled as she made her way to the tape line.

Sierra grabbed a ping pong ball, stood behind the line and waited as Grayson made an attempt at bouncing his into the trash-can. He missed, the kids laughed hysterically and began cheering, 'Sier-ra, Sier-ra, Sier-ra!' She tried to aim the ball the same way she would aim her nine millimeter pistol at the shooting range. She had been a Law Enforcement Security Police during her enlistment in the service, and she had an expert shooting record. 'Here goes nothing she thought,' and bounced the ping pong ball across the rug and directly into the trash-can. The kids went ballistic. Grayson could not stand being upstaged by a girl, especially this girl, he said, 'Give me another ball – let me show you how it is done!' He bounced a second ball and missed again, but at least this time it bounced off the edge of the trash-can. 'One more, give me one more,' he shouted laughingly, 'I am just warming up.' Grayson's third attempt at aiming the ping pong ball redeemed his manhood to some degree; he made it into the can.

Sierra was glad, she felt kind-of bad about making him look bad in front of his youth group, but not too bad. 'Okay buster, you got three tries, so I get three tries too,' she jeered. 'Give me two more ping pong balls.' Fearing she had built herself up to a challenge she couldn't meet, Sierra aimed nervously, then stopped and said, 'If I make this it will make your youth leader look bad, so maybe I will miss on purpose.' Everyone cheered and laughed, 'Okay, here goes nothing,' Sierra said as she bounced her second ping pong ball directly into the trash-can.

The brutish boy who offered to date Sierra before the meeting started yelled, 'Whoa! That's two out of three, Gray she already beat you dude!' 'Okay guys, one more. Let's see if she can go three-for-three,' Grayson said, as he too began to cheer Sierra on.

The room grew quiet, almost too quiet, as Sierra aimed the third ball at the trash-can. She bounced it in the same spot on the rug and it went directly into the trash-can for the third time in a row. Grayson instantly reacted without thinking. He grabbed Sierra like a rag-doll, lifted her feet off of the floor, and hugged her with his virile arms as if he had done it a million times. She wanted to stay there forever. She could feel his chest against her body and his face so close to hers that she could feel his breath. Grayson and Sierra both knew at that moment that something was happening, a God thing. The chemistry was too strong to deny. They just looked with an intense stare into each other's eyes, even if only for a second, it was enough. Then he put her down.

Sierra's mother always told her that, 'Actions speak louder than words.' Grayson's actions spoke volumes to her. She knew now that he too felt the overwhelming connection that had knocked her off balance and kept her there all day long.

As the kids went on to play the rest of the game, Sierra and Grayson attempted to cheer the teams on and act normal, but neither of them could stop glancing in the other's direction. 'How can I be in love with someone I have not even known a day,' Sierra pondered in her mind as she gave way to the reality that was in her heart. This was the guy. She just knew it was the guy she had been praying for. She could never have imagined that she would find him in the very place she burst her tennis-shoes to get away from after finishing high school. She would never have believed that God would answer her prayers when she felt so far away from his will.

The very reason Sierra joined the Air Force in the first place was to get away from there. She wanted to meet new people, see new places, and definitely find a husband one day without connections to *La Maison*. She was now convinced that God does have a sense of humor after all.

With this reality, Sierra tried to prepare herself to speak to the youth, knowing that Grayson would be listening intently to every word she said in an effort to learn more about this girl who was rocking his world the same way he had rocked hers. 'Um, Grayson, I am going to go grab a glass of water while they finish up this game,' she spoke bashfully.

'Okay, that's fine, we have five or ten more minutes, so go right ahead,' he said in thoughtful response. Sierra rushed out of the youth room and made a direct line to the bathroom. She wanted to check her hair, her clothes, her make-up, and her teeth to make sure she looked okay before becoming the center of attention, not for the youth group, but for Grayson.

When she got to the restroom, Alisa was there. 'Soooo, how is it going,' she asked. Oh my- Alisa, I am about to hyperventilate. He has been flirting with me, I really think he feels the same thing I am feeling. As crazy as it sounds, I think I love this guy. I never believed in love at first sight, but he has made a believer out of me! I can't even think straight,' she whispered excitedly. She told Alisa that Grayson thought she had gone to get water, but she really just had to get out of the room for a minute before she passed out from the pounding of her heart.

'It sounds like the real deal girl; I always told you when you know you know. Now you know. It is not something anyone can really explain, but when that match made in heaven happens, all doubt is removed.' Alisa said with assurance. 'Thank you! Thank you; so much, for not making me feel like I am a nutcase, Alisa,' Sierra said as she hugged her sister-in-law like never before. 'I have to get back in there, the game is just about over, and I have to go get a glass of water so he won't think I lied.' Sierra was anxious as she ran out the door of the bathroom toward the kitchen to get a glass. 'Relax, relax, relax Sierra, you have to come back to planet earth before you get back in that youth room,' she reprimanded herself as she hurried to the water fountain with a small paper cup she had found in the kitchen cabinet.

As she filled the cup with water from the fountain just outside the youth room, Grayson cracked the door and said, 'Are you about ready? Team two won the game.' 'Yes, I am coming right now,' she answered as she walked toward the door as Grayson held it open for her. She went into the youth room and sat in the same folding chair as before, anxious, but trying to seem calm.

'As I told you before, we have a guest speaker today. I have asked Sierra Bradley to come and share with you what it is like to live and work in the Air Force, especially from a Christian perspective,' Grayson gave as an introduction.

'Oh boy, how am I going to share life in the service from a Christian perspective when I have not exactly been living according to one myself? Should I be honest, knowing that Grayson will judge my actions, or should I sugar-coat it to make myself look good?' She thought.

'Without waiting any longer, Sierra, why don't you come now and share with us what is on your heart,' Grayson said as he began to clap his hands encouraging the kids to do the same. 'My goodness, I surely can't share what's on my heart today,' she thought, but she smiled and walked to the podium Grayson had placed back on the rug for her to lean on. 'Thank you so much, I appreciate that,' Sierra said in response to their applause.

'I pondered in my mind what aspect of life in the military the Lord wanted me to share with you today, and to be honest with you, until right now I really had no direction. There are so many different perspectives to draw from that I was having difficulty choosing just one. As I made my way to this podium, I believe the Lord spoke to me and wants me to share this with you. I joined the service to get away from 'life as I knew it.' I wanted to 'find myself,' and become my own person. I was tired of being told by my parents how I was going to do things, and when I was going to do things. I wanted to make my own decisions, even if they were mistakes. With that immature and selfish attitude, I did just that. I made decisions, and I made mistakes. I will live with those decisions, but I learned from them, and if you will listen to me tonight, you too can learn from my mistakes without having to make your own. God has a plan for each of us. That plan is in stone, and no matter how we try to run from it and do our own thing, He will have His way. When I ask myself why I went into the Air Force, I regret to admit that my answer is not, 'Because that is what the Lord told me to do.' When I met the guy I have been dating for the past two years, I regret to admit that I was not dating him because he was the guy God told me to date. When I bought the car that I have been driving since I started my job with the Law Enforcement Security Police Force at my Air Base, I regret to tell you that I did not buy it because that was what God told me to do. I guess what I am trying to say is, more than anything else I have learned while serving in the military, I realize today that if we make decisions according to our own wishes and desires rather than according to the desire God has for our lives, we will get off track – not sometimes, but every time. So if I can encourage you with anything tonight, it is this: Don't decide what you want for your life. Let God decide, and if there is even a shadow of doubt over any decision you are about to make, whether it be a small issue or a huge, life decision, don't make it. Never make a move in life, whether it is choosing a career, choosing a school, choosing a boyfriend or girlfriend, choosing a car to drive, or even just choosing where you are going to go for lunch tomorrow without first having that unhindered assurance that it is the choice God would have you to make. I could say a whole lot more, but that is the real message I believe God sent me here tonight to share with you.'

It's funny, the whole time Sierra spoke to the youth; she didn't look over at Grayson one time. She had not noticed that his face had lost all of its color. He was as white as a sheet, and in a mesmerized state.

Chapter Five

'Um, Grayson, that's all I have to say if you want to come take over that would be great,' Sierra said as she tried to figure out what he was thinking. 'Oh, um, yes... thank you so much Sierra, that was an amazing message. What do you guys think, does anyone have any questions for Sierra?' A few of the less shy kids asked questions about her expert shooting skills, and what it was like in basic training, but most were a bit shy. Sierra was confident that the message she was supposed to convey was delivered, and that was all that mattered.

'Ok then youth, you did a great job, I am proud of you for listening to Sierra with such intensity. Now, let's go outside and I will give you the surprise,' Grayson said. The youth peeled out the door as fast as their feet would take them. 'Just wait for me right there in the field, I will be out in a minute,' Grayson hollered as they ran. Sierra asked inquisitively. 'What is the surprise?' Well, really there isn't a real surprise he explained, 'I am going to spray them down with a water hose after I get them all in a line – then I have about five-hundred water balloons I am going to let them play with. They are going to love it, so if you don't want to get wet, I suggest you stay back,' Grayson laughed and went to get the hose.

'Grayson is a really fun person, on top of looking like Mr. America,' she thought. Sierra really didn't want to get wet; she was not into the whole water balloon fight with teenagers she didn't know thing, so she told Grayson she thought she would just go on back to her parent's house. 'Okay, well I have to head back to New

Orleans as soon as we are finished here; anyway, I have a class at eight o'clock in the morning. Thank you for coming tonight, I really enjoyed what you had to say. 'Oh, no problem, I enjoyed it. It was really nice to meet you; Grayson, you do an amazing job with these kids.' 'It was nice to meet you too. Hey, I will be coming back up on Wednesday evening. Maybe we could get together before church and talk a little bit. Do you think you could come a little bit early?' He asked. 'Sure, I can do that,' Sierra said as she thought to herself, 'this is funny, I haven't been to church on Wednesday night in years, but if Grayson wants me here, I will be here with bells on.'

Sierra headed to the main sanctuary to find her Mom. Judith was just about to walk out the door so she decided to wait for her in the car. As soon as she sat down and closed the door, she saw Grayson running over to the car. He knocked on the window of the passenger side door. Sierra rolled the window down with anticipation.

Grayson just stood there looking at Sierra through the car window for about thirty seconds. Sierra could tell he had something important to say, she felt chills over her whole body as she looked into his piercing eyes and waited to hear what seemed so pressing.

'Sierra, I feel like the Lord wants me to say something to you, and I don't really know why, but here it is: If there is a window in your life that is open to the world, in order for the Lord to fulfill his desire in you, that window must be closed. Now, I don't know if that makes any sense to you, but that is what God wanted me to tell you. God has something for your life, but you are going to have to give up your own agenda in order for him to give it to you.' With that, Grayson said goodnight and walked away.

Sierra was stunned, just when she thought the day could not get any more profound, Grayson came to her with words that pierced her very soul. She knew exactly what God was directing his words toward in her life, but it amazed her that Grayson heard from God clearly enough to know what to say. She knew what had to be done. She knew what God was saying. This truly was the beginning of a new chapter in Sierra's life.

She had to be finished with the parties, the friends, the idea that Christianity was only for Sundays, and most of all, she had to be finished with waiting for PJ to change. Sierra knew the phone would ring at eleven-thirty that night. She had to be ready to be honest with PJ. She had to tell him he was not the one for her. She had to tell him what just yesterday she never could have uttered, that she did not love him. She had to apologize to him for leading him astray, and making him think it was okay for a Christian to date a person who chose not to follow Christ. She had to put an end to her two year relationship on the same day PJ decided to finally say he loved her. What a day!

Though she knew it was the right thing to do. Though she was overwhelmed with the day's encounter, and felt love for a man she barely knew, Sierra was saddened. She really did love PJ. He was her best friend, like a wink and a smile. She would miss riding on the back of his bike, and hearing him call her his little baby-doll. She would miss his big black eyes with beautiful eyelashes so long they nearly touched his eyelids.

She would have to dismiss nearly every memory of life on the Air Base because most of her memories included PJ. He would drive through the main gate while Sierra was on duty, just to say hi! He would run across the parking lot just to be standing at the door when she got off of work. He would take her to concerts, and for long rides in the country with their leathers on, laughing at her helmet hair. His sweet kisses were also going to be hard to forget.

'If only he had realized earlier that he loved me, things would have been different,' she thought for only a second before she shook her head. 'No, no I can't go there! I have to remember that it was never God's will for me to date PJ in the first place. That was my desire, so God, please forgive me for making decisions based on my own wants and desires, help me to step into your desire for my life,' she prayed aloud.

Sierra battled with these thoughts for hours until the clock struck eleven-thirty. She waited anxiously by the phone, but it didn't ring. She waited five more long minutes, but it didn't ring. Finally; at eleven-forty-five, she decided to stop watching the phone and go to bed. She brushed her teeth, and went into her old bedroom. She could still see the stickers on the wall that she put there when she was in the third grade. She got in trouble for that. She could see the dolls in the top of the closet that sat on her bed when she was a child. She was glad to be back home, she was glad God was working in her life, but she was also unable to sleep because she couldn't stop thinking about PJ.

She felt really bad for him. She wanted him to be happy, and knew this was going to make him everything but happy. 'Lord, please, prepare PJ for what I have to tell him. When he calls, speak through me so that my emotions do not get in the way of your will, I need you...' about that time the phone rang. Sierra suddenly felt like she was going to be sick. 'That has got to be him, oh man I hope I can get through this,' she muttered as she ran to get the phone.

'Hello,' she said as she put the phone to her ear. 'Hey baby-doll,' PJ said with as much excitement as he could muster. 'I have been waiting for this moment all day long. What cha doin,' he said. Sierra could see his white smile and his cute little head bobbing when he said that, just as it always did. 'Nothing, I was just getting ready to go to bed when you called,' she replied. 'Hey, Guess What!' PJ exclaimed. 'What,' Sierra asked. 'I took leave for next week. As soon as I get out of this training, I am going to jump on my bike and ride all the way to Louisiana. I have something I want to give you,' PJ was overjoyed as he spoke those words. 'What could he possibly want to give me? Probably a ring,' she feared.

Sierra knew it was now or never, she was going to have to tell PJ the truth about what God had done in her life that day.' 'Um, PJ, I have something to tell you and I don't know how you are going to take it,' she began. 'What's that babe, I can take anything,' he said in response to her introduction.

'There is no way I can tell you what I have to say so that it will make sense to you, so I am just going to spit it out. I think I met the man I am supposed to marry today,' she said. 'Wh -what,' PJ said with a little chuckle as if he was waiting for the punch-line of a joke.

Sierra continued, 'PJ, I am not joking, and I owe you an apology. I am a Christian, and for the past two years that you have known me I have not been a very good one. You have not seen me going to church, you have not known me to be a person who prays and studies my Bible, and you have not known me to use discretion with my language. I have been a terrible witness, and for that I am sorry.

'I have only been home for a week, but today I went to church. My Mom asked me to sing the special during the morning service. You know I used to sing in an ensemble before we met. So; anyway, I agreed and when I got to the church I met this guy named Grayson Raines. As crazy as it may sound PJ, as soon as I looked at him I knew he was the man I was going to marry. I didn't even know his name. It was literally like cupid shot and arrow and hit me right in the heart. I...'

'Okay then,' PJ interrupted. 'Don't say anything else. I recognize rejection when it happens. Do you really think you can love a person that you have known for less than a day? Thanks for stealing two years of my life. I guess this is goodbye, oh and have a good life. You will never have to worry about hearing from me again,' he said with a disappointed tone 'I just called to say I love you.' With those words, he hung up the receiver. A dial tone sounded off in Sierra's ear.

Sierra closed her eyes in an effort to stop the tears from flowing, but it was useless. Her heart was broken. She had wounded her best friend, and now there was not a thing she could do about it. Sierra worried about PJ. 'What would he do now? Would he ever become a Christian, or would her association with him push him farther away from the Lord? She couldn't prevent the nauseated feeling she had at every thought of that dreaded phone call. She went to bed flustered, trying to ignore the aching in her heart and go to sleep.

She tossed and turned until she decided to pray, 'Lord, I am sorry for doing things my own way. I am sorry for making decisions without your guidance. It is my fault that PJ is heartbroken right now. If I had listened to you, he would not have come to this point. I would certainly not have dated him. I am sorry and I pray that you will strengthen him. Send people into his life who will be a positive testimony of Christianity for him. Please Lord, don't let him become bitter.'

Sierra didn't know how long she had cried and prayed for PJ before she fell asleep. Her last thought was, 'I will never hear from PJ again.'

Chapter Six

When she woke up, it was a new day. Not only because the sun had peeked over the horizon, but because she had decided to turn the page in her life story and move on. She could no longer live in the past. God was doing a new thing in her life and she knew she had to embrace it.

God placed Grayson in her path. It was no accident; even though he was a blessing she felt unworthy of. 'I need to just embrace the gift God has given me,' Sierra thought to herself before she climbed out of the bed to face the day.

Sierra not only needed to accept God's forgiveness, she needed to forgive her self. She poured through her mind with a flood of 'what-ifs' as she headed to the bathroom. She should have boarded a plane to Greece on the very day she drove her little car to Louisiana after her discharge. She had a choice to make. Stay in the Air Force for another enlistment period and go to Greece to guard the American Embassy, or take her honorable discharge and go home. She chose to go home. Something deep in her gut told her that was the right choice. She knows now that 'something' was God.

If Sierra were to be honest; however, she would have to admit that she also chose to go home rather than to Greece because she was reluctant to move six thousand miles away from PJ. 'What if that was supposed to work out,' was what she thought as she deliberated her choice.

That thought was more than she wanted to deal with at the time. 'If I go to Louisiana, at least PJ and I will be close enough to make a day trip and be together,' that was her reasoning.

But, today she did not need to consider that as her motivation. She recognized above all that God was fulfilling His plan for her in spite of her foolishness. This was not about PJ, this was not about Sierra. This was only about what God was doing that was out of Sierra's control.

'Whoa, Sierra, you look like you have been run over by a truck,' she thought as she walked around the corner of her old bedroom and caught a glimpse of her image in the back bathroom mirror. The mirror wrapped around the entire bathroom wall, giving no escape from the ghastly display. Her face was streaked with the residue of black mascara– apparently from the tears that fell from her eyes most of the night.

'Wow, Sierra, you forgot to wash your face last night. Love really looks good on you,' she said aloud as she laughed at herself. If her hair had been long enough, it would have been tied in knots, but since it wasn't, it resembled a rat's nest. 'A shower will do wonders!' She convinced herself as she pulled back the sky-blue shower curtain and turned on the faucet in the matching blue bathtub so that the water could get hot enough to start the shower.

'What should I do today,' she contemplated as she stood under the shower head in a steady stream of nearly blistering hot water. 'With a car payment due next month, I should probably think about finding a job. Hmmm, where would be a good place to start?' She wondered.

Sierra wanted to start school, but that possibility limited her job potential. She did not want go to college while working a fulltime job unless she absolutely had no other choice. Anyway, most 'real jobs' would require some sort of commitment. 'I will talk to Mom about it, maybe she has an idea,' she decided as she turned off the water and stepped out of the shower onto the fuzzy blue rug beside the toilet.

'What were they thinking when they built this place, she thought to herself as she looked around. The bathtub is blue, the toilet is blue, the sinks and countertops are blue, the walls are covered in mirrors, and the floors are a muddy brown color. Well, at least it isn't lime green and mustard yellow like in the kitchen at the church. I guess it could be worse,' she thought as she wrapped herself in a sky blue towel from the cabinet.

'Well, now that's better,' Sierra thought as she saw the refreshed image in the surrounding mirrors. He skin was blushing from the rejuvenating shower, but at least the mascara streaks had gone down the drain, and her head no longer looked like a pedestal with a bird nest sitting upon it.

Pulling on her purple footie pajamas and zipping up the front zipper, Sierra got tickled at herself again. 'You look like a twelve year old Sierra,' she thought. 'Well, one of these days that is going to be a good thing,' with that thought, she headed to the kitchen where Judith and Stan were already looking at the morning paper and sipping coffee.

'Daddy, do you see any good jobs listed in the classified ads? I need to find one before my car payment comes due again,' she said as she bounced over to where he was standing. 'Let's see,' he said as he began flipping the pages to find the classifieds. 'Uhhh, Pets, Lost and Found, Properties for Sale, Ahh! Here it is, help wanted, that's what we need. Umm, physical therapist needed, must have two years of experience, Nurses wanted, nope neither of those will work. Telemarketers, ticket salesmen, grocery store clerk, Sierra, why don't you just go down to one of those temporary work places and get a job through them until you find something you really like. They don't pay a whole lot, but at least you would be doing something until the job you are looking for comes open,' Stan suggested. 'He always seems to have a great idea,' Sierra thought. 'Ok, I think I will, thanks dad,' she said as she grabbed a couple of the giant, fluffy biscuits Judith had just pulled out of the oven.

'I need to call Travis today. Yesterday I fell asleep when he was supposed to call,' Sierra insisted. 'Yes, actually he did call while you were asleep, but he didn't want to wake you up. He said he would call back tonight or tomorrow. He is in the middle of a big training exercise on his base in New Mexico, so he isn't free to call just any time.' Judith explained.

'Oh, I hate I missed him, so it isn't a good idea for me to call him right now, I will just wait, surely he will call when he gets a chance,' Sierra said with regret. 'Thanks for the biscuits, they are really good,' she said changing the subject.

Judith asked Sierra if she wanted a cup of coffee, but Sierra laughed and told her that was one thing that would probably never change. She hated coffee when she was a kid, and she still hates it now. 'Whoever came up with the idea that you develop a taste for coffee as you get older must have been ninety years old with no more taste buds, that stuff is just nasty,' Sierra proclaimed with disgust. Judith and Stan chuckled with delight. They were so thankful to have Sierra back in their home.

'Okay then,' Sierra announced, 'I will get ready and go to the temporary job office today and see what they can come up with for me. After that, I will probably give Rachel and Trisha a call. I haven't seen them since I have been back. That reminds me, I need to go get a new phone today too. Anyway, we may go out for dinner and movie or something if they are up to it. I don't know if I will be here for supper, so don't worry about me. 'That sounds great honey, you need to spend some time with your friends,' Judith said in agreement.

'Here we go again, what should I wear? It's a job interview, maybe I should dress up a bit. I don't want to overdo it, maybe some slacks and a sweater would do the trick,' Sierra considered her options as she made her way to her suitcases.

'I need to get all of this stuff put up somewhere tonight. I hate to take over the closet, but I can't just leave everything in the suitcases either. I am sure mom and dad won't take offense if I unpack. I don't want them to think I am just going to move back in and take advantage of them after having been out of their home for four years. As soon as I find a 'real job' and get my feet on the ground I will find my own place, I am sure they will understand that,' Sierra trusted that they would. She decided she would discuss the matter with them after her visit to the job office today.

'Red, I think I heard that red is never a good color to wear for an interview, it is too ... well, flashy. I think it is best to wear gray. Let's see, what do I have that is gray?' Sierra thought as she looked through her better clothes. 'Well, here's a gray sweater vest, maybe that will work, it is really more of a charcoal color, so if I put a black turtleneck under it with some black slacks and a pair of leather boots that should do the trick,' Sierra felt confident in her choice of attire.

'Now, what are the chances that I can dry and roll my hair and it turn out looking exactly the way it looked last night? I think slim to none, but I am going to give it a shot,' she smirked as she looked once again at her towel-dried hair in the menagerie of mirrors.

'Do you need me to iron something for you Sierra,' her mother said as she walked down the hallway toward the back bathroom. 'Well, if you want to run an iron over these slacks that would be great. Thanks! I really appreciate it mom.

Sierra was not used to having someone to help her. It was nice. As Judith gathered Sierra's clothes off of the bed, she noticed the boots she planned to wear were a bit scuffed. 'Your dad will polish your boots for you while you get ready,' Judith said with sincere desire to help out. 'I feel so humbled, thank you so much,' Sierra didn't really know what to say, so a simple thank you would have to do.

Once the rollers were taken out of her newly dried hair, Sierra did the best she could to replicate the style from the day before. 'Close enough,' she sighed as she took one last look in the mirror before getting dressed in her newly pressed clothes and Marine shined boots. 'Mother, you don't have some kind of necklace I can wear with this outfit that would make it look more, I don't know, professional, do you?' Sierra inquired of Judith as she walked into the living room with her purse as if she was ready to go.

Sierra knew the answer to her question before she even asked it. Judith was a connoisseur of costume jewelry. She had an entire dresser filled with earrings and necklaces rather than clothes. Sierra was sure Judith would have something to fix her up in style. 'Oh, I am sure I do, let me just go see what I can come up with. Do you want silver, or black, or do you want to add some color to what you are already wearing?' Judith's mind began to spin with ideas. She loved to help. It seemed to make her day if she could make someone else's a bit brighter. That was just Judith.

'Um, I think maybe something silver and black would be good if you have it. A long necklace that would come down far enough to touch the top of the sweater would be good,' Sierra said. As Stan laced up his work boots, he asked Sierra, 'What kind of job do you think you will go for?' 'I don't know what they will even have to offer. I don't want to go work in a fast food place or anything like that. If I can get a job at a bank, or as a secretary, or something along those lines it would be my choice until something more permanent comes open,' she replied thoughtfully.

'You know you could go be a cop, or work at the post office or something like that and you would not lose your time in service, and all of that training,' he said. Sierra was waiting for that remark to come from her dad. She knew she could go back into Law Enforcement, but she really – really didn't want to do that. She felt inadequate looking like a little girl playing dress up in a police uniform. She was afraid that in the 'real world' people would not take her seriously. 'Halt! Who goes there?" sounds more like a wind up doll than a threatening remark from a law officer coming out of her mouth. 'Let me just explore my options before I go that route daddy,' she voiced in reply to his suggestion.

'Here you go sweetheart, I have red, orange, purple, silver and black. Pick whichever one you want, then you can have the rest of these too, you never know when you may need another color,' her mother had such a giving heart. She would literally give the shirt off of her back to Sierra if she thought she would wear it. 'Oh, mother, I don't need all of these, just let me borrow the silver and black one today, that will work out perfectly,' Sierra humbly replied.

'Okay, but if you ever need any other color, you know where to find them,' Judith said with a loving smile. Sierra really hoped her mom and dad never felt even a tiny sense that she was using them. She appreciated all that they were willing to do for her, but sometimes felt that she was asking too much. *Count your blessings. Name them one by one.* The words to that old song resonated within her soul as if they had dropped in her mind from nowhere. 'Okay God, I get it, you want me to just be thankful,' she thought as she looked up at the ceiling feeling as if she had been put in her place.

'Alright then, I am ready to go. Wish me luck,' Sierra said as she marched toward the door with her keys in her hand. 'You will do great; honey, you look like a professional, just answer their questions, do your best, and be yourself, that's all you can offer. God will do the rest,' her mother's words were encouraging, as usual. 'I love you, and I will see you guys tonight when I get home. If Travis calls, tell him that I am going to try to get a phone today, so I will catch up with him as soon as I can,' Sierra said as she rushed to her car.

Sitting in her car, Sierra took a long, deep breath before starting the engine. It seems that the rest of the world fades away every time she closes that driver's side door. 'It's just you and me God. I don't really know how to walk in this. You are going to have to teach me one step at a time. I want to please you from this day forward. Show me your way so that I can walk in it,' she prayed earnestly as she lay against the headrest of the driver's seat.

As if the voice was audible, she heard God speak to her at that moment. 'Sierra, if you want to walk in my way, you can start by cleaning out your glove box right now before you go another step,' the voice said. Sierra looked around, startled to see who was speaking to her. No one was there, at least no one that she could see. 'Oh my goodness, the Holy Spirit just spoke to me - literally spoke to me and told me what to do,' Sierra thought, on the verge of disbelief.

This was all new to her. 'Can the Lord really talk to me like that,' she thought. When suddenly the verse she had memorized, from Isaiah, Chapter 30, when she was a kid in Bible Drills, came to her remembrance. "Isaiah 30:2: Whether you turn to the right or to the left, your ears will hear a voice behind you saying, 'This is the way; walk in it,' Isaiah 30:2' The verse came back to her memory as if she had learned it only yesterday and had just stepped forward to recite it in a Bible Drill competition.

'Wow, I feel like I am in a whirlwind. It must really be the time in my life that God wants me to become more than what I have been. Okay, Lord, let's get that glove box cleaned out," Sierra knew the idea of 'cleaning the glove box out' had more significance than simply discarding the items that it contained. It meant letting go of what her flesh still held on to. 'God, if you are going to lead me to get this out of my life, I pray that you take the desire away from me completely right this very moment,' she prayed as she opened the latch.

A box of cigarettes fell out of the glove box and landed on the seat. This habit started in Sierra's life as a result of childish peer pressure, and had blossomed into a full-blown addiction during her time in the Air Force. This was that 'window' Grayson had spoken of the night before. She had no doubt. The window had already been shut on PJ, now it was time to shut this window of addiction.

Sierra picked up the unopened box of cigarettes, peeled off the wrapper, emptied the entire box into her hands, and broke them in half all at the same time. 'Satan, you are not going to control me with this addiction any longer, I give this to you Lord, and I ask you to forgive me where I have failed you for so long.' With that, Sierra opened the door, marched to the garbage can that sat beside the brick wall on the side of her parent's carport, and brushed her hands of it.

'The desire immediately left her," Sierra had heard so many horror stories of people trying to quit that she didn't know how she would ever manage to do it, but with her obedience, God instantly and completely lifted the desire for a cigarette. God healed the addiction while she sat in her car - instantly. The desire of her heart must have been stronger than the desire of her flesh.

Chapter Seven

"Psalm 51:10: Create in me a clean heart, Oh God, and renew a right spirit within me, Psalm 51: 10," yet another Bible Drill verse came to Sierra's remembrance as she drove toward the temporary job office. She didn't even want the radio on. It was as if Sierra wanted complete silence just in case the Holy Spirit had anything else to say. She wanted to be ready to hear it.

"Boy, it's only nine o'clock in the morning and it feels like I have been going for twelve hours," Sierra thought as she checked her hair, make-up, and teeth one last time before stepping out of her car and walking in the job office. A lot had happened in the past twenty-four hours; that was for sure. At this same time yesterday morning, Sierra was not the same person she was walking into that job office today. 'Lord, open the job that you would have for me, not the one I would necessarily choose,' she prayed.

'Hello, my name is Sierra Bradley, I am interested in applying for a job,' she said to the refined lady who sat behind the receiving counter in an airline stewardess type of uniform. 'We are so glad you are here Miss Bradley, my name is Tanya and I will be happy to get you started with an application this morning. If you will take this questionnaire, and fill it out, it will give me a general idea of where your skills, and interest lie, if you have any questions feel free to ask.' Tanya said as she handed Sierra a clip-board.

Name, address, phone number, date of birth, social security number, most of the top part of the form was routine information.

The bottom; however was the beginning of about one- hundred personality type questions. 'Man, they must be weeding out the terrorists with this questionnaire,' Sierra laugh quietly inside as she began to write.

It took Sierra about fifteen minutes to complete the questionnaire, then another fifteen minutes of waiting after she turned it in. Finally, Tanya said, 'If you will come with me,' compelling Sierra to follow her lead down the narrow hallway. 'We will take a timed test of your typing skills. It seems from the questionnaire you filled out you may be suited for an office type job. Does that sound like something you would be interested in?' 'Yes, actually that would be perfect,' Sierra responded with a positive attitude, trying not to show too much excitement. 'Be professional, but be natural at the same time,' she told herself.

Sierra felt a bit rusty on her typing skills since she had not worked with a computer on a regular basis, but she knew she could type well enough that she would not embarrass herself. 'We will give you a battery of three tests and then we will take an average word count from all three. Each section consists of a paragraph that contains words, numbers, and symbols. Your formatting skills will also be taken into account for some of our job postings, so you will want to keep that in mind. Errors will count against your word count, so it is better to type a bit slower and show accuracy than it is to have more words with errors. Does that make sense?' Tanya asked as she set the test pages before Sierra.

'Yes, I understand. Just tell me when to start and I will get to it,' Sierra attempted to say with confidence though her heart was beating out of her chest, and her hands were shaking from nervousness. 'Calm down Sierra, you can do this. There is nothing to worry about, the worst case scenario would be a job at a fast food place,' Sierra kidded herself as she waited for the timer to start. 'When you are finished typing all three paragraphs, hit the timer button to stop the clock. And...start,' Tanya said as she flipped the switch on the digital timer.

The paragraphs were long, almost a full page each, Sierra was afraid she was going to lose her place while she typed. She remembered the teacher telling her it was important to learn to type without looking at her fingers, but she lacked confidence. Every few words, she just had to look down and make sure her fingers were where they were supposed to be. 'Oh, Sierra, you are hitting that backspace button too much,' she thought as she worked for perfection in every sentence.

Sierra stopped for just a second, took a deep breath, and reminded herself that she was not in control of this test, God was. She needed to let him have it. With that reminder, the second and third paragraph did not bring as much stress as the first. 'And…stop,' Sierra said as she reached for the timer button.

Twelve minutes and twenty-two seconds, that was her time. She wondered if that was a good time or not. Tanya said, 'Well, the time looks great, now let's just check and see how many errors you have. Each error will add to your time. Sierra was not expecting Tanya to find very many errors, she had been careful, actually typing slower than usual to make sure it was as close to perfect as possible.

'If you will wait right here, I will check it over on my computer,' Tanya said. A long five minutes later, Tanya came back with a smile. 'Yep, girl, you ripped that test up. I only found two errors in all three paragraphs,' Tanya boasted. 'So now I will send your information to the places that require such a skill, and they should be contacting you before the end of the week. If you don't hear from someone by Friday, give me a call, but I don't think that will be the case.' 'What kinds of places will you be sending my information to,' inquired Sierra. Lawyer's offices, banks, doctor's offices, and things like that, they are usually the ones looking for a receptionist or a secretary with typing skills, and they usually pay better than the other jobs too, so you should do fine.' Tanya encouraged Sierra as gathered her things and headed to her car.

'I really need to get a new phone,' Sierra thought as she prepared to drive out of the parking lot of the job office, 'But maybe it would be a wise decision to wait until I have a secure job before I sign a two year contract.' she thought.

'I wanted to call Rachael and Trisha, I guess I will just have to stop by their houses and leave a note if they aren't home,' Sierra decided that would be her best bet. Rachael lived closer to the job office than Trisha did, so Sierra went there first. As she pulled in the driveway, it was surreal to see the baby swing on the tree, a stroller on the carport, and a bicycle with a baby carrier on the back. Rachael got married about a year after she graduated from high school. Presley, her baby girl, was about fifteen months old.

It seemed strange to Sierra that her best friend was married with a baby, had her own house, and was about to graduate from college with her teaching degree. 'I wonder if that is where I would be if I had made different choices,' she thought. She wrote Rachael a note and stuck it in the door:

> *March 5*
> Mrs. *Rachael Ragsdale, (still seems weird to me* ☺*)*
> *I came by but you weren't here. I am home now —*
> *so if you have any free time, give me a call. I would*
> *love to see Presley, and spend time with you. Just let*
> *me know. I don't have a phone here yet, so just call me*
> *at my Mom and Dad's house.*
> > *Tell Jason I said hello too!*
> > *XXOO*
> > *Sierra —*

'Well, let me go see if I can catch Trisha at home. She works at the dentist office, so if she isn't home, I could probably catch her there,' Sierra thought to herself as she pulled out of Rachael's driveway. 'Boy, I sure hope I catch her, I need to tell them what has happened to me in the past twenty-four hours. I need them to celebrate with me, or tell me I am crazy, or something!' Sierra was starting to feel alone and anxious. Silverside Apartments — that's where Trish lives. Trisha Warren had been Sierra's sidekick since first grade. She was in nursing school at LSU, working on the side as a dental assistant three days a week.

'Ok, Silverside, this is it, she used to be in A-3, now she lives in apartment D-7, let me see if I can find it,' Sierra thought as she drove around the complex looking at the numbers posted on the doors and buildings. H, I, J, no, I must be going the wrong way; these letters are going up, not down. Sierra turned around and drove in the opposite direction, J, I, H, G, F, E, D…

'There it is, D." she bragged to herself. She parked her car and walked to the doors looking for number seven. 'Here it is,' when Sierra found it, she rang the doorbell. She waited and rang it again, but there was no answer. Disappointed, she decided to just leave Trish a note too.

> *Hey Trish –*
> *This is Sierra; I stopped by to tell you what has been going on in my crazy life for the past couple of days, give me a call when you get a chance. I don't have a phone yet – so just call Mom and Dad's house. Maybe we can go to dinner or catch a movie - - let me know.*
> *Love ya – S xxoo*

'Ok, so no one is home this morning, who can I talk to?' Sierra pondered in her mind that may be home right now that would care about what was going on in her life. 'Mmmm, maybe Alisa is home, boy I hate not having my phone, it sure makes things difficult!' she thought as she pulled out of Trisha's apartment complex and headed to her brother's house.

Grant and Alisa lived on the other side of town in a house they built when they first got married four years ago. Alisa is only a year older than Sierra, even though Grant is almost thirty. They don't have any children yet, Alisa wanted to finish nursing school first. She will graduate in about six weeks.

'She would understand how I feel about Grayson being older than me. Please be home Alisa – I am going to go crazy if you aren't' Sierra thought. She drove up the driveway and saw Alisa's car in the garage. 'Thank you Lord!' she shouted out loud as she parked.

Sierra rang the doorbell, and poked her head in the front door, 'Hello, is anybody home?' She said before she went inside. She heard Alisa yell from the back room, 'Yes, I am here, come on in, I will be right out.' Sierra sat in a barstool in the kitchen and waited for Alisa to come out.

'Hey, what's up,' Alisa said as she rounded the corner putting an earring in her left ear. 'I was just about to head out the door to meet a friend for lunch, you wanna come with us?'

'Well, I hate to be a third wheel, I just wanted to talk to someone about what happened last night, and you were on my list of people who care,' Sierra said laughingly. 'Well, come go with me, we can talk in the car on our way to meet Annette. We are going to hit lunch traffic anyway, so it will take at least twenty minutes to get there, then we can talk on the way back too if you want.' 'You're the best, Alisa,' she said.

'Why don't you move your car so I can pull out, then you can park yours in the garage while we are gone,' Sierra did as Alisa ordered. 'Do you have your phone? I wanted to just touch base with Mother and let her know where I am and how the job interview went,' Sierra asked as she got into Alisa's car. 'Yes, I have it. What job interview? You didn't tell me you had a job interview today,' Alisa whined.

'The truth is; I didn't know I had one until this morning when Daddy suggested I go to a temp office and find a job that would tie me over until something more permanent came open. I really want to go to school, so I don't want to strap myself down with a full time job commitment, but I need something that will generate enough income for me to pay my car note, get a new phone, and maybe an apartment in a month or two.'

'Hold on a second, let me call Mother real quick,' Sierra stopped Alisa just as she was about to speak. 'Hello,' Alisa could hear Judith speaking on the other end of the line. 'Hey Mom, it's me. I am with Alisa. We are going to get a bite to eat. I went by Rachael's and Trish's but they were both gone, so I came by to talk to Alisa and she invited me to lunch. I just wanted to let you know so you wouldn't be worried,' she said. Sierra's Mother always appreciated knowing where she was, even though she was not a kid anymore. 'Okay honey, thanks for letting me know,' Judith responded and hung up the phone. Talking on the phone was not her favorite thing to do, but sometimes it was necessary.

'So, what's up is everything okay?' Alisa said as soon as Sierra hung up the phone. 'Now it is, but I am not going to lie to you, the past twenty-four hours have been the most surreal of my entire life. I told you last night at church that I think I love this guy Grayson, and I don't even know him. Last night, just as I was trying to go to sleep, the phone rang, it was PJ. Alisa, he called to say he loved me. He called to say he had taken leave to come to Louisiana because he had something he wanted to give me. I am almost sure it's a ring. I feel so bad – I cried myself to sleep over it, but the only thing for me to do was to tell him the truth.

'What did you tell him?' asked Alisa. 'The truth, I told him the truth. I told him that I think I have met the man God wants me to marry, as crazy as that sounds, and that if I can have feelings for another man, then that is confirmation in my spirit that he is not the one I am supposed to be with for the rest of my life. I told him that I was sorry for leading him to the wrong impression of what Christianity is truly about, and that I have not been a good example for him. Then, before I could say anything else, he said that he would never talk to me again, but that he had called to say he loved me. With that, he hung up the phone. I tried not to cry, but it was no use, it hurt! He was my sidekick. We were best friends. He called me his baby-doll. Alisa I love PJ, I still love him, but I realize after what happened yesterday that I am not in love with him. Only God can match people up in such a way that they are truly in love, and to our understanding it makes no sense. The way I feel when I even think of Grayson makes no sense to me whatsoever! I just know that it is God.

'You did the right thing Sierra, you know that don't you. You did the right thing, and now PJ in God's hands just the way you are. God has a plan for him too. He is not going to lead him astray. You have to believe that and let go of your guilt.'

'Well, that's not all of the weirdness that has happened to me since I told you how I felt about Grayson last night. After church, he came to my car window and said the Lord had given him something that he had to tell me, but he didn't exactly know why. He said, 'If there are any windows open to the world in my life, before God can have his way with me, I would have to close them,' or something along those lines. I knew immediately what he was talking about, but Alisa, how did he know to say that to me? It had to be directly from God. Then, this morning, something even more unusual happened. If I didn't believe it, I would think I was going nuts. I got in my car to head to the job interview at the temp office, and I heard someone speak to me and say, 'Clean the glove box out.' Now I looked around and there was no one there. It was the Holy Spirit! I actually heard the Holy Spirit speak out loud to me in my car and tell me to clean my glove box out.

What no one knows is that my glove box is where I keep my secrets, things I know are not right, that I don't want everyone to see, but that I haven't been able to let go of until now. So, I opened the glove box, broke all of my cigarettes, threw away everything I was holding on to, and I was instantly set free. I have been delivered, completely and totally delivered from addiction, and a lifestyle that did not glorify God. If God wants me to be a part of Grayson's life, and I think that he does, I am ready for it. Two days ago I wasn't, but now I am.

I even went for a job interview at the temporary job office this morning and God spoke to me while I was taking the test. I feel so different inside. I feel like my whole purpose for living and being on this planet has come to a new place – even today. I feel light, I feel free, almost like I am not even myself. I have truly been emptied out – and now God is going to fill me with what he wants. I am excited and scared at the same time.

'Wow! What a testimony! I don't know if I have ever heard of God doing a complete turnaround in someone's life literally overnight, but it seems like that is what has happened to you. I can see why you are overwhelmed. It means a lot to me that you would feel comfortable enough to share all of those intimate details with me, I want you to know that,' Alisa said in response to Sierra's confession.

'No, thank you! Thank you for being there for me-for not judging me - and for your willingness to listen to my crazy life stories. Of all people, I know I can count on you, and that is a blessing,' Sierra humbly admitted.

Chapter Eight

'I really enjoyed lunch. That was a great Mexican restaurant. Thanks so much for inviting me, but most of all, thanks for listening. I love you Alisa,' Sierra said as she drove out of their garage headed back to her parent's house for the night.

Sierra rehashed the happenings of the day as she began the twenty-minute drive back to her parent's house. Her anxiety had settled down, her heart was more free, she knew that when she turned on the radio and began scanning the channels for a good song. Sierra was so thankful Alisa was there.

'Way down yonder on the somethin' another - no one knows how much that dog named – blacky means to me...' Sierra sang at the top of her lungs to as many words to the song as she could remember. The ones she didn't remember, she just threw in her own words, she just felt like singing.

When she made it to the house, Stan and Judith had already gone to bed. Sierra was tired, and she was glad. She was not ready for another sleepless night. She jumped back in that blue shower for a few minutes, this time she washed her face too, threw those footie pajamas back on, and curled up in her bed. She was asleep before she finished praying.

'Good morning, good morning, good morning, it's time to rise and shine. Good morning, good morning, good morning, I hope you're feeling fine, good morning, good morning, good morning, it's time to start your day, so raise your head, get out of bed, stand up and shout hooray! Rachael sang with enthusiasm in an effort to wake Sierra up. Oh my goodness, some things never change! What are you doing Rachael?' Sierra chided as she pulled the pillow over the top of her head. 'Get up you sleepy head. It's almost nine o'clock. We have a busy day!' Rachael said. 'We are picking Trisha up and going to New Orleans for the day so get up and get dressed. Didn't you get our messages, we called last night and left you messages about what we were going to do.' Rachael said as she pulled the covers completely off of the bed. 'Ummmm, no, I was so tired when I came in last night that I didn't even notice. I'm sorry! I can get ready really fast. I took a shower last night, so I just have to fix my hair.' Sierra grumbled. 'Just throw a hat on for crying out loud, open your eyes and look at me. I sure didn't doll up for you. Just get dressed and let's go.' Rachael persisted.

Sierra slid out of the bed and into the bathroom, she was about to brush her teeth when it dawned on her, 'Grayson was in New Orleans, maybe he could meet them for lunch. But, would that be too forward, too awkward?' She would ask her Mom.

Throwing her clothes on, deciding to just go with jeans and a t-shirt with a windbreaker since it would probably be pretty warm in New Orleans, and throwing on an LSU cap, Sierra was ready to go. 'I will put my make-up on in the car on the way there,' she said. 'Hold on just a second, I need to ask my Mom something real quick,' Sierra said and then knocked on Judith's bedroom door.

'Come in – I am just drying my hair,' Judith called out. 'Rachel and I are going to pick Trish up and go to New Orleans for the day. I wanted to let you know before I left.' Sierra said respectfully. 'I think that will be fun, thanks for letting me know,' Judith replied. Sierra proceeded to ask her Mother if she thought it was too forward, or awkward to call Grayson while they were in New Orleans and see if he wanted to have lunch with them. Sierra was sure that Rachael and Trish would want to meet him after she finished telling them her story.

'Ummm, let me think about that one for a minute,' Judith said with a puzzled look on her face like she had some better idea. 'What if I call Pastor Allen and tell him that you are going to be in New Orleans today; then he can call Grayson at the seminary, tell him you are there, and see if he asks where you will be. If he does, Pastor Allen can tell him what you are doing, and give him the option to show up where you are - thinking you won't be expecting it.'

'Well Mom, you are quite the schemer aren't you,' Sierra said. 'How will he know where to tell Grayson we will be?' she asked. 'Silly, Pastor Allen will tell Grayson you are going to be some place at some particular time; then he will call me with that information. I will call you on Rachael's phone, I have her number in my caller id and you make sure you 'happen' to be there at that time,' she explained.

'If you don't hear from me, then it didn't work out.' Judith said. 'Well, that sounds like a plan,' Sierra said with nervous excitement still not believing that her mother is playing cupid. Sierra asked Rachael if she was sure she had her phone as they headed out the door. She could not wait to tell her on the way why that was such an important issue on a day like this. 'Yes, I have it, no worries,' said Rachael as she glared at Sierra.

Sierra knew exactly what that glare meant. Rachael was offended that she would even suggest that she had not brought her phone. She was a perfectionist about those things. 'Anyway; Rachael, who's keeping Presley today?' she said in an effort to let the air out of the situation. 'My mom and dad wanted to take her to the zoo, so I thought today would be as good a day as any, that way we could spend the day together without worrying about her getting tired.' Rachael announced with pride. She always liked to have a plan, and when her plan worked out it was always that much better for her, and everyone else around her too, for that matter.

Rachael picked up her phone as she drove out of the Bradley's driveway. She called Trish to let her know they were finally on their way, making sure she included the fact that Sierra was still in the bed upon her arrival, and the fact that she had not heard their messages the day before. Sierra felt incompetent, as usual. Rachael had not changed one bit, but Sierra loved her for it.

'So, I can't tell you how glad I am that you finally came home from the Air Force,' Rachael began. 'I have had so many days that I would have loved to just sit around and drink tea, or go to a movie, or something, just anything, but you were nowhere around,' she continued. 'Now, if I have a day, at least you are close enough that I can at least see your face once in a while,' she finished as she reached over and grabbed Sierra's cheeks and shook them between her fingers as if to make a sweet gesture of friendship.

'Trish is waiting for us at the end of her driveway. I think she is anxious to see you,' Rachael and Sierra laughed out loud. Trisha was not known for her patience; that was certain. She wasn't as demanding as Rachael, but she definitely did not like to wait. Rachael was; of course, joking about Trish being at the end of her driveway. It was an inside joke between the girls from when they were in high school. Rachael and Sierra had been about fifteen minutes late getting to her house one Friday night, and when they finally showed up, Trish was standing out by the road so that they would not have to take the time to drive up the driveway. She was tired of waiting! It has been a joke amongst them ever since.

When they arrived at the apartment complex, Trish was not at the end of the road, but she was standing at the door waiting to lock it when they pulled up. She pulled the door shut and ran to the passenger side of the car to steel a hug from Sierra. 'Ohhhhh, it's so good to see you again. I have missed you soooo much!' Trish squealed as she squeezed Sierra with all of her might. 'It is just not the same without you here, I am so happy that we could all take the day and go to New Orleans. It will be so much fun.'

'Get in the car Trish, we need to go, you can talk all the way to New Orleans,' Rachael said as she put the car in reverse.

'So, Sierra, what's been going on with you? We need to get caught up,' said Trish from the back seat. 'Well, that's a loaded question, Trish. Do you want me to give you the short version or the long version?' Sierra responded with a playful tone.

'Just give us the scoop on PJ, that's the part we really want to hear,' Rachael said without hesitation. Sierra started from the beginning, knowing she had a two hour trip to New Orleans to tell her story. 'Where should I begin,' she said aloud as she pondered the idea of starting the whole story off with the phone call from PJ.

'Well, a lot has happened in the past two days that you are not even going to believe. By the time I get finished with my story you will probably think your friend has finally gone over the deep end.

PJ and I were doing fine when I left the base last week. I was headed home; he was leaving out for a three week training course for the 82nd Airborne. We had every intention of meeting half way when he got out of training so that we could see each other. It would only be about a three hour drive for each of us, so it wouldn't be too bad.

Well, he called me Sunday night and said that he was going to take leave for the week after his training and ride his bike down to Louisiana because he had something he wanted to give me, and he wanted to meet my family, and he said that he thought he loved me.' Sierra reminded Rachael and Trisha at this point that PJ was not the 'meet the family, drive to Louisiana to give you something' type.

'I truly didn't know how to respond to him, so I told him to call me back that night. You see, if he had called me the day before, I would have been on cloud nine. I would have been in town looking at wedding rings without a doubt.' Sierra explained.

'Awwww, that is sooo sweet,' Trish interjected from the back seat. 'But that's just it, he didn't call the day before, and that morning, before he called something transformational happened in my life. 'I went to church with my Mom to sing the special in the morning service, and I met this guy named Grayson Raines.

The only thing I know to say about him is that he made me a believer in love at first sight. I don't know, something just happened to me the moment I laid my eyes on him, and it has not stopped. I think it has changed my life forever. I have had encounters, but never one like this. I truly believe that my chance encounter with Grayson was a God thing. He was the reason I couldn't talk to PJ. He rocked my world.' Sierra admitted.

'Oh, I am sooo jealous,' Trisha said with a sigh. 'What was it that got you all love struck?' Rachael asked. Sierra tried to explain that it wasn't his cover model body, or his piercing blue eyes, although those definitely drew her attention, it was something supernatural that drew her to him. It was God, and that was made clear to her over the course of the following twenty-four hours of 'cleaning her glove box out.' Sierra took time to explain to her friends what that cliché was about.

'I broke it off with PJ, I broke my cigarettes in half and threw them in the garbage, I emptied my secrets out before the Lord, and now I am free. I am forgiven, and I am fillable with what God wants to pour into me. I really believe that Grayson is a gift from God that I had to be ready to receive, so God has taken the past two days of my life and purged me of everything 'me,' so that he can start over with His plan for my life,' Sierra spilled it out to them.

'So, when can we meet this cover model guy?' Trisha queried. 'Well, actually there is a possibility you can meet him today if everything works out.' Sierra said with a grin. 'How today, we are going to New Orleans,' Rachael prodded. Sierra jeered back at Rachael telling her that it just so happens that Grayson Raines is already in New Orleans and if he chooses to do so, we have the opportunity to be in the same place that he will be today at a given time.

'What in the world are you talking about Sierra,' Rachael begged. Sierra explained the plan that Judith had concocted before they left her house. So, just keep your phone turned on. If he decides to meet me somewhere, my mom will call your phone. She will tell you where we need to be, and at what time. If not, we will just enjoy the day anyway. Sierra said that, but she was really thinking about how crazy her nerves were going to be all day long waiting for that phone to ring.

'Well what does he look like,' Trisha could not stand to be left in the dark, she wanted to know everything. 'He is not quite six feet tall if I was guessing. He has brown hair that is kind-of wavy, his eyes are crystal blue, and when he stares at me I feel like they are going to burn a hole through me.

He looks like Mr. America, I know you think I am joking, but I am not. He is like two- hundred pounds of solid muscle. He looks like a super hero. I had to pinch myself when I first met him to see if I was dreaming. I am still not sure what he does to get his body like that, I hope to ask him the next time we meet. He asked me to show up for church early tomorrow night. He wants to talk.

'How old is this guy?' Rachael asked. Sierra truthfully did not even know how old he was, she told Rachael that she supposed he was about 26, but she was not sure. She said that she knew he was out of college, because he was attending the seminary, but she was not even sure what his degree was in and when he graduated, or from what University. Sierra felt a bit embarrassed that she was telling her friends she had fallen for a guy and she didn't know anything about him, not even know how old he was.

'All I know is that I am drawn to him like a piece of metal to a magnet. After two years of dating PJ, my entire focus is totally and completely shifted and it was of no coercion of my own.' Sierra explained.

'No matter what happens from this day forward, God used Grayson to change my life, to get me back on track for the plans he created me for. I really believe that God intends for me to marry him, but if I am wrong, he still will be a forever part of my testimony because the moment I met him my life was literally transformed from the inside out. I see the world differently.

I see my life differently, I make decisions differently, my desires are different; my focus is different. I guess it is safe to say I am a totally new person. You remember that verse from Bible Drills, '2 Corinthians 5:17: If any man is in Christ he is a new creation, old things are passed away, and behold, all things become new. 2 Corinthians 5:17.'

Well that is my new life story. That is exactly what happened to me yesterday, the old 'me' is gone and God has totally remade me and set me on a new course. That's the only way I know how to explain it.'

Sierra's story was interrupted by the sound of the LSU fight song roaring from Rachael's purse. 'Oh, it's my phone, can someone grab that, I can't get it while I am driving,' Rachael demanded. Sierra dug into the side pocket of Rachael's purse, pulled out her phone, and noticed it was her Mom calling. She was so excited she could hardly speak, 'Hello, Mom, is that you?' Sierra answered nervously. 'Yes, it is me. Hey, Grayson did call back and Pastor Allen told him that you would be at the River Walk near the fountain at two o'clock this afternoon. So – make sure you are there and don't act like you knew he was coming.

'Thank you! Mother, you are a genius! I owe you one! Well, I owe you a bunch, but thank you so much! I am so excited!' Sierra could hardly contain her excitement.

Chapter Nine

'It Worked!' Sierra blurted out with uncontained joy, 'He called and want's to meet me today! We have to be at the River Walk fountain at two o'clock. Sierra's hands were trembling and she could barely catch her breath.

'You've got it bad girl,' Rachael said jokingly as she poked Sierra in the arm. Rachael remarked with certain confidence that if she was this overjoyed with the thought of meeting a guy at a fountain that she had only met one time, this was a guy she just had to meet. 'We'll be there girl, don't you worry about that. And we will be there on time Trisha!' Rachael eyeballed the backseat as she threw out that sarcastic remark to Trish.

'Well what I want to know is does he have a brother,' Trisha commented. 'If he can sweep you off of your feet and send you floating in the clouds, I want his brother!' she laughed.

'That's the funny thing, I don't even know!' Sierra answered honestly.

'So, where do you want to go first?' Rachael enquired as she began to make plans for their day. 'If we have to be at the fountain at two o'clock, then we need to work the rest of our day around that meeting. What if we go to the IMAX - and the aquarium first, then we can work our way toward Jackson Square, and end up at the River Walk before two o'clock,' Rachael laid out her schedule. 'Sounds like a plan to me,' Sierra responded gleefully.

By the time the girls reached the IMAX it was eleven thirty. 'We have two hours before we have to be at the fountain, Rachael commented.' Trisha put her two cents in, 'Why don't we spend about an hour here, grab a bite to eat, then make our way to the fountain,' There is a great little Cajun restaurant on the River Walk, if you guys want to go eat lunch there, we can just stay until it is time to walk over to the fountain to meet Mr. Right.'

Sierra was taken aback by the sights and smells of New Orleans. The Jazz music blaring from the intercoms, the path tiled with bricks with messages from the sponsors carved in each one, the tall buildings, the trolley cars, and the smell of beignets all made Sierra feel a sense of pride in where she was from. 'Louisiana is truly a cultured place,' she thought as she looked around and saw things that she had never really noticed before.

'When you live in this culture day-in and day-out there are a lot of things you take for granted.' she reflected. Sierra realized as she walked toward the ticket booth for the aquarium that there was not another place on earth quite like New Orleans.

Sierra enjoyed the time in the aquarium with Rachael and Trisha, but she would have to admit that her thoughts were a bit preoccupied with her two o'clock appointment. 'I wish I had taken time to fix myself up a bit,' she thought. 'I hate for him to see me looking so shabby. For peat's sake, I'm wearing a cap on my head! Well, at least I put some make-up on in the car – it can't be that bad,' she tried to convince herself.

Anxious with anticipation, Sierra voiced out loud, 'Do you guys think I look too, I don't know, frumpy to be meeting Grayson at two o'clock? Maybe I need to get something else to wear, or get my hair fixed, or something.' Rachael and Trisha countered her notion simultaneously with a resounding, NO! 'You are one person I know who could crawl out of a bag and look cute, he needs to see you for who you are – and more often than not – this is who you are. You look like a doll, you wear that cap well, rock it girl, just the way you are!' Rachael showered Sierra with compliments.

'You don't need to even think about what you are wearing for another second. Let's go on to the restaurant,' Trish encouraged them, 'We have seen these fish a million times, we need some girl time just sitting around the table, and we only have about an hour before Grayson is supposed to show up?' Rachael and Sierra agreed. Trish put her arm around Sierra, grabbed her shoulder and pulled her close as she told her how glad she was that she could be a part of this new 'thing' God was doing in her life. 'See what we would have missed if you had taken that job in Greece!' she said.

'Yes, see what I would have missed! It's amazing that God really had a plan for me and I could not even see it. 'Thank you; Lord for directing my steps, even when I wasn't asking you to. There is no telling where I would have ended up if I had made the decision to go to overseas.' She pondered these thoughts in her mind as she visualized her possible future with Grayson.

Making their way to the River Walk, Rachael began to list off the possible restaurant choice in the area. 'There's fast food, but we don't want that. There's a little café-like place that serves sandwiches, but I know Sierra doesn't want that. There's that little Cajun place I was talking about, and there is an Italian place around the corner. What sounds good?'

'Nobody cooks Cajun food like my Mother, so I hate to go pay good money to eat second best – why don't we try the Italian place, I could use some good mozzarella sticks!' Sierra figured it was her day; she might as well make a choice.

'That sounds like a plan to me, but if we go there we just need to watch the time a little bit closer because we can't see the fountain area from the restaurant.' Rachael clarified. 'Okay then, let's do it, Rachael, just set your phone on the table so we can watch the time. As long as we head to the fountain by about a quarter till we should be good, that gives us a good forty five minutes to chat, and eat.' Trish calculated.

The Italian restaurant was perfect, the lunch rush was just about over, the setting was quiet and quaint with candles on the tables, and the hostess directed the girls to a corner table away from the hustle and bustle in the entrance. Rachael stuck with what she was familiar with and ordered Lasagna, Trisha tried the lobster ravioli, and Sierra went with her all-time favorite, shrimp Alfredo, and of course, an order of cheese sticks.

Sierra changed the subject, 'So, enough about me already, tell me what's going on with you guys. You are both getting ready to graduate soon – how exciting. I am so proud of you.' Rachael was finishing out her last semester, and Trish had one more to go before she had her degree. Sierra fought the temptation to covet what they had accomplished. Rachael seemed so happy with the family life, and had accomplished so much in the middle of it all. Trisha was following her dream to become a nurse and was already considering jobs at the largest hospital in Baton Rouge.

Sierra felt a little bit inadequate, as if she had not done much worth bragging on in her own life. She was a proud veteran, had completed the police academy, and was considering the possibility of love, but her accomplishments paled in comparison to her friends, or at least that was how she felt.

'So, tell me about Presley, what's it like being a mom?' Sierra directed her attention to Rachael. 'Well, our plan was for me to finish my degree before we started having children, but God had other plans. It has been a challenge at times to keep pressing on in school, especially during the first six months after Presley was born, but I would not trade her for the world. She is such a miracle blessing that I stand in awe of every day of my life.

Jason has been a blessing too, I have had to take some night classes since Presley was born so that we didn't have to leave her in a daycare. I keep her during the day while Jason works, and he keeps her in the evenings so I can go to class. It has not always been the best thing for our marriage, but we know it is a temporary situation, six more weeks – woo-hoo! Rachael expressed from her heart.

'She is a great mom,' Trish interjected. 'I love it when I get to babysit, but I don't think I will ever be as good of a mom as Rachael is. Presley practically worships her.' Trish said. 'Now, Trish, all babies cling to their moms at this age, that is just normal.' Rachael said humbly. 'Trish thinks that Presley worships me because every time I call her to babysit, Presley cries when I leave. I have tried to tell Trish not to take that personal, but she just can't seem to let go of it. Presley loves Trish, but I am just her mama. That's all.'

'Ok we have mozzarella sticks, and three sweet teas with no lemon,' the waiter read from his order to ensure he was at the correct table. 'Yes, that's us, thank you very much,' Trish said as she slid the cheese sticks in Sierra's direction. 'Your orders will be up shortly, in the meantime, if you need anything feel free to ask, my name is Charles,' he said cordially.

'Ohhhh, these look amazing, Sierra said as she cut into the first cheese stick. 'Well I think that Charles the waiter guy looks pretty amazing too, and he is not wearing a wedding ring,' Trish expressed her opinion without regard to the cheese sticks. 'If you can meet a guy and fall in love in one day, why can't I,' she prodded.

The girls looked at Charles a bit differently when he brought out the Caesar salads. They noticed his blond hair that was combed back perfectly to one side, his tan skin that made them think he must spend a lot of time outdoors, and his neatly pressed uniform which suggested he took pride in the way he looked. He was tall and slim, but not too slim. 'Not bad, Trish, I have to agree with you he is pretty cute,' Sierra nodded. Growing more nervous as the clock on the table ticked, she was glad things were running smoothly and the time was not getting away with them. By the time Charles brought the food to the table, it was only twenty after one.

'Perfect timing,' she thought. After eating as much as she could with her nerves in a jumble, Sierra asked for a box, excused herself, and went to the restroom. She wanted to make one last check in the mirror before her accidentally purposed meeting took place by the fountain. When she felt confident that things were as good as they were going to get, she went back to the table. By the time the checks were cleared and they were headed to the fountain it was ten till two.

'Now listen, you know this is supposed to seem like a surprise. I am not supposed to know Grayson is here. So; act natural, don't embarrass me, okay!' Sierra could feel her stomach in her throat, she half regretted what little she did eat. 'You will be fine, let's just go walk around the fountain, and then we will sit down on one of the benches so that we can watch the area. You let us know when you see Grayson and we will try to act natural,' Rachael said in an attempt to control the situation.

As the girls rounded the corner on their way to the fountain, Sierra stopped in her tracks. 'Oh my goodness, he is already here!" Sierra exclaimed. 'Where, where is he,' Trish questioned anxiously.

Sierra felt exactly the same way she had felt the first time she saw Grayson in the church fellowship hall when she had to go back outside and catch her breath. She scooted back around the corner, pressed her back against the wall, and took a deep breath in an effort to calm her nerves.

'Psalm 37:4 – Delight yourself in the Lord and He will give you the desires of your heart. Psalm 37: 4.' God brought this verse to her remembrance as she stood against the wall. 'It's that voice, that voice behind me telling me which way to go,' she thought. 'Be anxious for nothing,' she thought.

'He is wearing a white polo shirt and a pair of red shorts. If you look around the corner you will see him standing by the fountain.' Sierra said as she breathed slowly trying to bring her blood pressure down a notch before walking in his direction. 'You are kidding me – right,' Trish said in an exasperated whisper. 'He looks like a model.' "I told you guys he was way out of my league, but God must not think so,' she explained. 'He looks like that, AND he is a Christian – there is hope for me after all,' Trish recounted. 'And anyway, he is not out of your league, quit being so hard on yourself Sierra!' Rachael verified.

'So what should I do, just walk up and act like I don't see him and hope he sees me, or should I just bravely walk over and say, 'fancy meeting you here' what a coincidence?' Sierra sincerely inquired of them. 'What do I do?' She almost cried.

Rachael was obviously the level headed one of the bunch so she took control. 'Let's just casually walk toward the fountain. We will talk about beignets, and the River Boat, the aquarium and we will stop over by the saxophone player. We will just act like we don't see him. Remember, Trish and I have never met him, he will not be suspecting us so we can watch him with no problem. We will walk in the other direction on purpose so you don't have to be looking right at him. That will give him a chance to approach you rather than you approaching him.' 'Sounds like a plan to me,' Sierra said shyly.

Grayson was leaning against the fountain with his back to them, as if he expected Sierra to come from the other direction. He was watching the roadside thinking that was where she would make her entrance. 'He is just as nervous as you are,' Trish said as she witnessed Grayson fixing his shirt, straightening his belt, and running his fingers through his wavy hair. 'He has changed his 'pose' three times since we walked this way, and he just took a drink of water. I think it is amusing. Boy if he is half as nice as he looks you hit a jackpot!' Trish maintained.

'Let's go listen to the guy on the sax.' Sierra said as she pulled her friends in his direction. He was on the other side of the fountain from Grayson, so she figured if they made their way over there he would see her from across the courtyard. 'I cannot breathe,' Sierra admitted, 'I feel like I would do well to find a seat.' They found a bench near the saxophone player that was positioned perfectly for Grayson to see them if he would just look that way. Rachael and Trisha kept a watchful eye on him as Sierra tried not to look in his direction. She was afraid of making eye contact. She didn't want him to suspect that she knew he was coming.

It didn't take but a minute or two before she heard his voice from across the courtyard, 'Oh – hey! There you are! Sierra, Pastor Allen told me you were going to be here this afternoon, so I thought

I would come over and say, 'Welcome to New Orleans.' Grayson shouted as he made his way over to the bench where she was sitting.

Watching him walk sent chills up and down Sierra's spine. She wondered what she had done to deserve a chance with a guy like him. 'He is perfect, and his eyes are like diamonds,' whispered Trish as she tried to compose herself. Standing up from the bench, Sierra yelled back at him, 'Oh my goodness, what are you doing here,' feeling a little fake since she knew full well what he was doing there. She wondered if she should shake his hand, or hug him, or just do nothing.

'I was talking to Pastor Allen this morning. Your Mom told him you were going to be in New Orleans today and that you were going to be near this area at about two o'clock, so I thought I would drive over and take a chance on running into you.' He finished his sentence just as he reached their vicinity. Sierra was thankful he broke through the awkward ice and reached right over and gave her an innocent hug. She breathed in his cologne as he pulled her close, and it was all she could do to back away.

'Oh, um – Grayson, these are my best friends Rachael and Trisha, Trisha and Rachael, this is Grayson. I met him this past Sunday. He is the youth pastor at *Flowing Creek Church*, where I was asked to sing,' Sierra introduced them as if it were the first time the girls had heard of him. 'It is really nice to meet you,' they said in unison. 'Oh my goodness, now what do I do, he looks so stunning, and I look like…well, I am not going to go there,' Sierra's thoughts were racing. 'We were just thinking about going for some beignets, do you have time to walk with us?' she gave the invitation as if that were the plan all along.

'Sure,' he said while looking down at his watch, 'I have a class at four o'clock, but other than that, I don't have anything else to do.'

Chapter Ten

'So, what have you been doing today?' Sierra asked reservedly. 'Well, I had a seven thirty class; then I went to the gym, got a bite to eat, cleaned up, and headed down to the River Walk to meet you.' He answered with confidence.

'Yes, I can tell you work out,' Trisha said boldly. Sierra thought she would die at that remark, but she had really been thinking the same thing, so she went ahead and ran with it as she rolled her eyes at Trish behind Grayson's back.

'Do you go to the gym every day?' she asked. 'Actually I go twice a day; usually, once in the morning before class, and again in the evenings before dinner. Today I missed my morning workout, so I snuck it in after class.' he explained. 'What got you into that,' Rachael inquired.

'I have been competing in power lifting for the past few years,' Grayson explained in a very humble way. It was obvious he didn't want to brag. 'What kind of contest did you win...? Mr. America,' she retorted with a serious, yet jesting chuckle. She was teasing, but would not have been surprised if his answer was, 'yes.' 'He definitely would have a shot,' she thought.

'I actually placed fourth in that competition last year in Atlanta because I hurt my back in the beginning of the meet,' he answered back. 'You placed fourth in the Mr. America competition, are you kidding me,' Trisha responded unbelievingly. Grayson laughed timidly as he told her he was not kidding. 'How did you get to that point,' Rachael asked. She was a stickler for details.

It was obvious that Grayson felt a bit uncomfortable talking about his accomplishments, but he answered anyway. 'Well, I won the Mr. Tennessee competition, so they sent me to Nationals, and that was where I hurt my back,' he began.

'See, after I won State, God spoke to me and told me that I was finished competing. I knew he wanted me to go to the seminary and follow Him in ministry, but I wanted more than that. I argued with God telling Him that I had found something I was good at, and asking Him why he wouldn't allow me to pursue it. Even though in my heart I knew that God did not want me to compete anymore, the doors of opportunity kept opening. I had corporations ready to sponsor me, I had the Olympic committee watching me, and I was invited to compete in the National competition after I took Tennessee.

I felt like it was God since there was no way I should have been winning against the guys that I was classed with. They all used steroids, and I decidedly never did. It would make them all angry because the only 'juice' I had before a competition was prayer, and I always won. I realize now that I was only winning because God had his hand on me to win. I know that because when I went to the Nationals, the first time I went to lift the bar I pulled my back. I dropped the weights, and lost a ton of points.

I ignored God, and went on with the remainder of that competition anyway, and I finished fourth. I still had invitations to compete in the Olympics, and sponsors ready to sign me, and honorable mention in mainstream magazines, but I knew if I went that route I would be out of God's will. I spent three days seeking the Lord, and all he would tell me was that He had already made His will for my life evident, and I needed to quit trying to avoid it. So, here I am a seminary student and youth pastor at a little country church in *La Maison*, Louisiana. How's that for a story,' he jeered.

Rachael, Trisha, and especially Sierra were moved to tears by Grayson's story of obedience. He had a chance at millions of dollars and to be an Olympic champion, yet he listened to God and followed that direction for his life. Sierra didn't think her feelings for Grayson could creep any deeper into her being, but now she wondered just how deep they would actually go. 'God, if this is not the man you have for my life, please don't let my feelings go any deeper, I don't know how to deal with. I am trusting that this is your will, but if I am wrong, please guard my heart because I am falling fast!' she prayed to herself.

'So you still work out, but you don't compete,' Trish said in an effort to break the silent awe they all felt. 'Yes, that's right. I have been working out for so many years now that it has become a way of life, a routine. I can't imagine not going,' he said in defense. 'Wow, I am impressed,' Rachael exclaimed. 'I have never met anyone who was going to the Olympics before, or even who had a chance to go to the Olympics. That's just the neatest thing ever, I feel like I need to ask for your autograph, almost Mr. America,' she laughed.

'Well, almost only counts in horse-shoes. That's what my Grandpa always says,' he said in response to her remark. Grayson was from a town in middle Tennessee that was even smaller than *La Maison*, as it turns out. He seemed so cultured, but beneath that masculine frame, he was just a great guy with a regular life, and a family about as normal as anyone else's, trying to follow God.

'So, do you have any brothers or sisters?' Trish asked as she winked across the table at Sierra. He explained that he did not have any sisters, but he has two brothers. Trish asked him if his brothers were married, and if they work out too. Sierra was ready to throw her drink on Trish to make her shut up, but Grayson had a great attitude. He told her that they were not married, but one was dating someone pretty seriously, and he was the body builder. His other brother was not into the whole gym scene.

'So, how did you end up in New Orleans, and in *La Maison?*' Rachael asked another practical question. Sierra was really glad that all of these questions were being asked. She was finding out a lot of things about Grayson that she really wanted to know.

He responded, 'I knew God wanted me to go to the seminary, so I searched out which ones were available, I visited around to several of them, and to be honest with you, when I came to New Orleans it was on the bottom of my list. I wanted to go where it wasn't so hot. But when I was staying here over a weekend visit, something happened that changed my mind.

Sierra was intently listening. She too wondered how Grayson had come to be in the very place that she would happen upon him when she should have been on a plane to Greece.

'I stood in the guest-room on campus one evening,' he said. 'I was looking out the window watching the rain. I had the application for the school in my hand and I threw it on the table beside the cracked window. I told God that I did not like it here, that I wanted to go to just about anywhere but here, and that was when I heard him speak to me.

Sierra couldn't believe Grayson was describing the Lord speaking to him the same way she had experienced his voice the day before. 'What did He say,' she asked in fascination.

'He called me Jonah,' Grayson replied. 'I didn't know what that was supposed to mean, or maybe I did know, but I didn't really want to hear it, so I closed the curtain and decided to lie down on the bed to go to sleep. When I closed my eyes, it was as if the Lord gave me a vision. I could see myself standing out in the rain, dripping wet, and weary, on one side, and over on the other side, I could see the sun shining, and a beautiful meadow. It was like God was telling me that I could make own my choice, but the blessings would not be there for me if I did.

At that moment, I jumped up from that bed, went over to that table, and filled out the application. Before I left the campus the following day I had already been accepted for the spring semester.

'So, what about *La Maison*, how did you end up there?' Trish asked while stuffing her mouth with a beignet. 'Well that is also a pretty interesting story, he admitted.'

'I moved to New Orleans at the beginning of January because the semester started on the 20th. I knew that I would need to find a ministry job so that I could get some experience under my belt. The registrar's office has a list of churches that are looking for Pastors and Associate Pastors, so I got a copy of that list. I really didn't want to start out with a pastorate since this whole ministry thing is new to me, and a lot of churches want their pastor to be married, so I looked into a few of the Associate requests.' Grayson explained.

'I went and preached at three different churches. Two were in Mississippi, and one was in the southern tip of Louisiana, almost in the Gulf of Mexico - literally. I didn't feel like they were the ones for me, but I was waiting for the second one in Mississippi to call me back. If they would have called, I probably would have gone there. Before they did though, my friend Alex came to me one Saturday night late – about seven weeks ago and said he was sick. He was supposed to be preaching in view of a call at a church in *La Maison* the next morning and wanted to know if I would go in his place. I already had a message ready for the other church, just in case, so I agreed. He gave me directions and I drove up the next morning.

When I finished preaching, the church had a time for questioning, and took a vote. I didn't even realize what was going on. I thought I had just gone to fill in for Alex. Before I knew it, Pastor Allen came out and said that the vote was unanimous – I was their new Associate/Youth Pastor. I didn't know what to say. But everyone seemed really happy, so I just said okay.' Grayson admitted bashfully.

'So, you were supposed to be in the Olympics and Sierra here was supposed to be in Greece when you met each other, isn't that ironic,' Trish spouted off at the end of his explanation. Sierra kicked her under the table. 'Yes, that is about the sum of it Trish,' he answered.

'Okay, so I just have to ask,' Rachael chimed in. Sierra cringed a bit with anticipation of what other revealing question may be about to come to the table. 'How does a guy like you not have a girlfriend, you are about the most eligible bachelor I have ever met,' she said without reservation. 'Oh my goodness, you did not just say that out loud to him in front of me,' Sierra felt sick to her stomach, yet anxiously awaited his answer.

'That's a funny question,' he said before explaining that he did have a girlfriend before he moved to New Orleans. 'At the time the Lord spoke to me about giving up the world of competition, I knew that all of the things that went along with it would have to go as well. The girl I was with had been heckling me to marry her for about three years. Something deep inside of me would not allow me to give in to that. I know now that it was God protecting me from making the biggest mistake of my life,' replied Grayson.

'If I had gone with my feelings I would have married her, and never known God's true plan for my life. Every time I even tried to think about asking her to marry me something deep in my gut just would not let me do it. We were both psychology majors, and had a lot in common, but once we graduated, and God wanted me to go to the seminary, I was certain she was not the person He meant for me to spend my life with, so I broke up with her,' he answered in such a way to assure them that he was confident in his decision.

'Wow, that's amazing,' Rachael said with a look of awe on her face. 'Too bad for her,' Trish added. Sierra just sat stunned at the flood of information pertaining to Grayson that had filled her brain over the past hour. If she wasn't in love before he showed up, she knew she was now. 'Can I just say that you have got the most beautiful eyes I have ever seen,' Trish threw in there on top of her 'too bad for her' comment.

'Just ignore her, she is crazy,' Sierra said to Grayson in Trisha's defense. "No, it's fine, I appreciate that Trish," he said in reply to her compliment.

'Well, girls; it has been nice spending time with you, but it is about that time. I am going to have to go now if I am going to beat the traffic going back across town and make it in time for my class, and Sierra; I will see you tomorrow – right?' He said with a wink and a click of his tongue. 'Yes, that sounds like a plan to me,' she said with a flirty grin. 'I look forward to it. It was nice to meet you

Rachael and Trisha, please be careful driving home,' he said – then turned and walked away.

Rachael and Trisha overpowered Sierra with comments as soon as Grayson walked away. 'Shhhhh,' Sierra hissed, he will hear you, at least wait until he gets to his car. 'You did good honey,' Trish said, 'I can't find one thing wrong with him.' 'He is like a miracle that God dropped out of heaven into New Orleans just for you,' Rachael included. 'Who ever heard of a story like that? Neither one of them is supposed to be in the state of Louisiana right now, much less sitting around this table getting to know each other. I think maybe this really is a 'God thing, and the fact that he looks like, well almost was Mr. America is only a bonus!' Trish concluded.

Chapter Eleven

'Let's go shopping! I need something to wear tomorrow night!' Sierra said with zeal.

'Sounds like a plan to me,' Trish said as she grabbed her purse.

The girls went into the River Walk Mall and shopped until they were beat. They had so much fun trying on expensive clothes that they would never have a place to wear. Mardi Gras masks and ball gowns, costumes and coats, it was truly a girl's day out. In the midst of it all, Sierra even managed to find a new outfit that would not be too dressy, yet would look nice for Wednesday night's meeting with Grayson. She found a pair of white jeans and a red sweater that had little braided flowers for buttons. It was perfect. She then found a pair of red shoes that matched it perfectly. She went home from New Orleans feeling more ready than ever for the next encounter with Grayson.

'It has been great spending the day with both of you. I can't wait to do it again. I will come by this week and see Presley,' Sierra said as she got out of the car at her parent's house after the trip home from New Orleans. 'We love you, have a good night,' Trish yelled out the window as Rachael drove out of the driveway.

Sierra laughed inside as she thought about everything that the day had accomplished. She couldn't help but think that when Rachael woke her up with that annoying little jingle, she would never have dreamed it would be the start of spending the day with Grayson in New Orleans. She was beginning to feel like a puppet on the end of a string that God was controlling. 'I guess that is how you want it to be,' she said out loud as she looked up toward heaven.

'Sooooo, tell me all about it,' Judith said as soon as Sierra walked through the door. 'Yeah, tell us about Grainey, Stan interjected from the other room,' her dad had always spouting off little mocking statements with regard to guys she liked. Sierra remembered one time when she was in about tenth grade and had just started to go on dates, Justin came by to pick her up to go to the movie. He walked in the living room wearing knee length shorts. Sierra was wearing a knee length skirt with leggings. Stan said, 'Well it's interesting to see that you will both be wearing a skirt to the movies tonight.' So, she was used to it.

'It went really well,' she began. 'When we got to the fountain, Grayson was already standing there waiting on me. We walked around behind him so we didn't seem to notice him, and sat down across the way. He finally saw me, came over and met Rachael and Trish. Then, we went to get beignets. He only had about an hour to spend with us because he had a class at four o'clock, but I sure learned a lot in that hour.

Rachael and Trish kept asking him personal questions about how he got so buff, where he went to school, and why he didn't have a girlfriend. He was so nice about it – and answered every question they asked, she said, giving them an overview of the visit.

'Well...what did he say,' Judith could hardly stand to wait any longer. He said that he was a competitive power lifter and almost won the National championships last year, but he hurt his back and came in fourth. He was invited to go to the Olympics, and had a girlfriend that he broke up with before he came to New Orleans,' just to give you the details. 'Oh, and he said that he really didn't want to be in New Orleans, but God basically spoke to him and told him this was where he needed to be. And, get this, the day he came to your church in view of a call, another guy was supposed to be there instead of him. His friend got sick the night before and asked Grayson to go in his place.'

'Well, it sounds like Grainey is right where he belongs, that's really good,' Stan said with a cynical, yet lighthearted tone. 'That sounds like something you would see in a movie,' Judith suggested. She analyzed the situation realizing that Sierra was not supposed to be out of the service, Grayson was not supposed to be out of competition, and *Flowing Creek* should never have called him to be their Associate Pastor, but all of the above had taken place because of God's orchestrating their lives like a jigsaw puzzle being pieced perfectly together.

'If she only knew the half of it,' Sierra thought as she listened to her Mother's reasoning. Sierra knew that not only was God piecing together the geographical puzzle for her and Grayson, He was also piecing together the spiritual and emotional pieces.

It was almost overwhelming for Sierra to realize that in much the same way that the Lord had been doing a miraculous work in her life, he was also working miracles in Grayson's life. God had turned her away from PJ, and protected her from marrying him. He had done the same for Grayson with his girlfriend. He had turned her away from things that were displeasing to Him through speaking to her in an audible voice. He had done the same thing for Grayson. He had directed her path away from where she wanted it to go and led her to *Flowing Creek Church* this week. He had done the exact same thing for Grayson. Even a few months ago neither of them would have believed they would be here today, but God saw to it that they were. This was a surreal revelation for Sierra.

'No one called me today about a job did they,' Sierra inquired. 'No, not that I know of,' Judith responded. 'Well, the lady at the job office said that I should hear something by the end of the week, so if anyone calls, please let me know.' Sierra pleaded.

'Goodnight honey, we are going to go to bed, it is getting late.' Judith said as she and Stan scampered off to their bedroom. 'Okay, goodnight – I love you,' she responded lovingly.

Sierra plopped herself down in the recliner and reflected on the dreamlike circumstances her life had revolved around for the past few days, and even before that without her realizing it. It was more than she could really grasp, but she knew it was reality. It was comforting for her to realize that Grayson was also in a state of awe with how God was directing his steps. She remembered another Bible Drill verse that applied to that perfectly, "Psalm 119: 105, Thy Word is a lamp unto my feet and a light unto my path. Psalm 119: 105." She was overwhelmed with the idea that God really does direct our lives in the way He wants them to go, and we make a choice to follow that way. All of those verses she learned reluctantly as a kid were making more sense to her now. She was realizing for the first time that all of those words are not just words, they are actually alive. 'God breathes through them, He really does,' she reiterated.

Chapter Twelve

Sierra woke to the chiming of a Grandfather clock that rested on the mantle above the brick fireplace in her parent's living room. It was nearly morning. She had fallen asleep in the recliner with all of the lights still on. 'It's still dark outside, I had better try to go back to sleep before the sun comes up or I never will,' she said as she stumbled to the back bedroom.

Still in her clothes from her trip to New Orleans, Sierra fell into the bed and was asleep before she even thought about changing into her pajamas.

'Sierra...Sierra honey, the phone is for you,' her mother announced as she came to the bedroom door. 'You slept in your clothes. You must have been tired,' Judith said as she handed her the phone.

'Hello,' she said attempting not to reveal that she was still half asleep to the person on the other end of the line. 'Hello, Miss Bradley?' Sierra heard a woman's voice. 'Yes, this is she,' she replied as she sat up in the bed. 'My name is Lucille Watson, I am calling from Trust Savings Bank about a job application you filled out at the temporary job office earlier this week, are you still interested in a job?' 'Yes – actually I am, I am glad you called,' Sierra replied anxiously.

'We have an opening for a position in our vault if you would be interested. It is a temporary position; however, if the person we hire is efficient and knowledgeable, it could become more permanent. If you would be interested, we would like to meet with you tomorrow at ten a.m.' she explained. 'That sounds great,' Sierra said in response to her offer, 'Can you tell me where you are located?'

'Yes, we are in the double towers off of Main Street, two streets over from the Capital building in downtown Baton Rouge. Are you familiar with the area?' 'Yes, I am sure I can find it with no problem, thank you,' she said respectfully. 'Just go to the receptionist when you walk through the main doors of the first building and she will direct you. We look forward to meeting you tomorrow,' Lucille concluded. 'Thank you, I look forward to meeting you as well,' Sierra said before she hung up the phone.

'That was a lady from that big bank downtown by the levee. She said they have a position open in the vault and want me to come for an interview in the morning.' Sierra told her Mother as she scurried into the kitchen. 'What in the world would I do in a vault,' she wondered. 'I thought all they put in there was a bunch of money,' she said. 'Well, in a bank that size they probably have safe deposit boxes, deeds, important papers, and stuff like that locked away so that no one can bother them, and – in the event of a fire - they would not burn up.' Stan explained as he grabbed his lunch before heading out the door to work.

'Yes, I guess that makes sense,' she agreed and told him to have a great day. 'So, what are you going to do today Mom?' Sierra asked. 'I don't know – I thought about going into town, but I think I have just about decided to sit in the living room and do a lot of nothing today, we have church tonight, so I may just take it easy,' she said as if she had been considering it all morning and had finally come to a decision.

'That sounds good to me,' Sierra said, I think I might just take myself right back to bed for another hour or so. 'Well there is nothing stopping you, unless the phone rings again,' Judith joked. Sierra responded with a quick 'if anyone else calls - take a message' and made her way back to the pillow-top. 'Hmmm, I will just lay here for about an hour, then I will get up,' Sierra pondered as she quickly nuzzled into the covers and went back to sleep.

Three hours later Sierra was jolted awake by the sound of a slamming door, and someone rushing down the hall. 'Get up and get ready, we have to go to the hospital, something is going on with Andrea and the baby,' Judith said in a panic. Sierra flew out of the bed, jumped in the shower, and was ready to go in less than twenty minutes. 'What's wrong,' Sierra said as she raced to the car with her Mom. 'They don't know. She was cramping really bad this morning, so Josh called the Dr. and they told her to get to the hospital immediately. They are afraid she may be having a miscarriage,' she sadly announced.

'Oh man, Lord please, reach down and touch that little baby right now. Please – whatever is going on inside of Andrea's body, calm it and settle her storm. They need you right now God, more than they need doctors. You are able to do far and above what we can even ask or think. Thank you Lord!' Sierra prayed as her Mother drove quickly toward the hospital.

By the time Judith and Sierra arrived at the hospital and inquired about Andrea, she was already being admitted into a room. 'The doctors said she was trying to go into pre-mature labor, like her body was rejecting the pregnancy. They are going to give her an IV with magnesium in an effort to stop that from happening. She is thirteen weeks, so they think it may work, if she was farther along it probably would not. They did an ultrasound and the baby looks fine, so pray they can get her contractions stopped.' Josh said with fear in his voice.

Andrea cried as she lay in the hospital room with the IV hooked to her arm. 'It feels like fire is burning through my body,' she explained. 'But if it will save the baby it will be worth whatever I have to do.' she acknowledged. Sierra held Andrea's hand and prayed for the calming presence of the Holy Spirit to fill her room and comfort Andrea and Josh as they faced this trying situation. She was glad; more now than ever, that she had made the decision to come home rather than stay in the service and take that job in Greece.

Judith called Pastor Allen to have him add Andrea and the baby to the prayer connection so that the congregation could be praying for them. He prayed with her over the phone; then told her that Grayson was on his way to the house and they thought it would be a neat thing if Sierra could come for an early dinner with them before church at around four o'clock. 'I will let her know, I am sure she will be happy to come,' Judith said with a smile.

'Let who know what,' Sierra said inquisitively as she recognized the grin on Judith's face was directed toward her. 'Grayson is on his way to the Allen's house. Sabrina is cooking dinner and wants you to join them at four o'clock before church. I guess everyone is in the matchmaking business these days.' She laughed.

'What was that all about,' Andrea said with a grunt as she attempted to adjust her pillow so she could see who she was talking to. Judith explained to Andrea that a lot had transpired since the Sunday evening service. She told her about Sierra's meeting in New Orleans, about Grayson's giving up the Olympics to follow the Lord, and about her invitation to dinner with him this evening. 'Sounds serious,' Andrea declared as she tried to muster a smile through the medication that was making her head feel dizzy. 'Yes, it does,' agreed Judith.

Sierra was bubbling in the corner of the hospital room, but tried not to seem too excited, after all, it was a serious time for Andrea. Sierra had strong faith in her prayers; however, and when she prayed for God to calm the storm inside of Andrea's body and save the baby, she just had no doubt that was going to happen. It wasn't too long before Andrea fell asleep. Josh lowered her bed and adjusted her pillow in an anxious effort to help out, then sat nervously by her side. 'At least she isn't hurting anymore. I was really afraid she was going to lose the baby,' he divulged.

About that time the nurse came in to check her vital signs and IV. 'If you had not come when you did, this would have turned out differently. It looks like they were able to get the contractions stopped before any damage was none,' she announced. 'Praise the

Lord,' Judith said as she let out a sigh of relief. 'The doctor will be in later to give you more details, but for now, she needs to rest, so we won't bother you – but if you need anything feel free to call. Just hit the nurse button on this remote and we will answer you.' She explained to Josh. 'Thank you so much. We really appreciate it,' he said in reply.

Josh encouraged Judith and Sierra to go on home. He said there was no need for them to hang around the hospital since all Andrea was going to be doing was sleeping. He told them that her parents were on their way, and he would call when they heard from the doctor. 'Okay then, we will go, but if anything changes, you let us know, and if you need us for anything at all we will be here as quickly as possible.' Judith insisted.

'Okay Mom, I love you, and thank you for being here,' Josh said as he hugged her and walked her to the hallway. 'Thanks Sierra, I appreciate your prayers!' he said to her as she followed Judith out the door. 'I have a job interview downtown in the morning, I will stop when I am done,' she said. 'We will look forward to it,' Josh replied as he slipped back into Andrea's room.

'It's almost one o'clock. You wanna go get a hamburger or something?' Judith said with an inviting look in her eye. 'Sounds like a plan,' Sierra replied, 'Let's go!' 'There's a great little restaurant in the mall,' she continued. 'It's like a smorgasbord where you choose a meat, two veggies, bread, and a dessert out of several choices. Aunt Eva and I go there all the time when we are out.' Judith suggested. 'Okay, that sounds really good to me. I don't want to eat too much though, remember I am supposed to go dinner at four o'clock at the preacher's house.' She said giddily.

'Fried chicken or hamburger steak,' they both look really good to me Sierra thought as she passed over the red beans and rice that was the special of the day. Fried shrimp for Judith, there is never a question what she will order if that is on the menu.

Once their trays were loaded down, Sierra laughed. 'So much for not eating a lot, this is enough food for two people,' she joked. Sierra could not resist the mile-high coconut pie with perfectly browned meringue on the top. Judith could never get out of the line without a hot, fluffy yeast roll to go with her shrimp, and of course a huge glass of iced tea and another with only ice. Some things never change and Sierra was glad!

Once they were stuffed, they decided to walk around the mall a bit before going home. They still had about an hour before they would need to head back for Sierra to get ready for her dinner. She was glad she already knew what she was going to wear, but as she looked around the mall she picked out a few more things that would have been suitable. She bought one dress that would make her feel good about herself on Sunday morning. Having been in the service for so long, and not attending church the way she should, Sierra's inventory of dress clothes was slim to none. If she was going to date a preacher, that would have to change.

It was a classy looking dress, navy blue, fitted, but not tight, sleeveless with a light sweater to go with it. 'I guess I need a pair of shoes that will go with this. Do we have time to look for some now or should I come back tomorrow?' She asked. 'Ummm, it looks like we have about thirty more minutes before we have to head to the house. If you can look quickly, I think we have time.' She encouraged. Sierra looked in the shoe department of the very store she bought the dress in and found a perfect pair of dressy sandals with a silver strap across the top. She was ready.

'Okay, so let's get home so you can get ready girl,' Judith said looking at her watch with haste. 'Sounds like a plan to me,' Sierra tittered as they rushed toward the exit.

Chapter Thirteen

By the time the Bradley girls made it home it was almost three o'clock. Sierra had about an hour to get herself together before going to Pastor Allen's house to meet Grayson. Josh called as she got her clothes out to say that Andrea was going to be fine. The doctor came in and explained that the magnesium had helped. Her uterus was relaxed, but to be on the safe side they are going to keep her on the IV for a couple of days. Andrea was going to have to take it easy for the remainder of the pregnancy. If she had any more spells like this one she would end up on bed rest for the duration of the pregnancy.

'We should send some flowers now that we know she is okay,' Sierra told her mom. 'I am going to go by there tomorrow after the job interview, I will pick some up,' she decided.

'That will be great, get a little bear or something to go with it,' Judith said in agreement.

'Now go get ready, you don't want to be late,' she said as she pushed Sierra lightly toward the back room.

Sierra fixed her hair, this time a little different than Sunday. She decided to pull the sides back with a barrette - just to change things up a bit. She touched up on her make-up, but decided to wash it off and start all over again. It still looked pretty good from the trip to the hospital that morning, but she wanted to feel fresh... so, she started over.

'Now – that's better,' she thought as she finished off the job with a touch of caramel-pecan colored lipstick. With that, she put on the new outfit she bought in New Orleans with Rachael and Trish, and was ready to go. 'So, I guess I will go on over there,' she told Judith as she noticed the clock. 'It's about a quarter till four, if I leave now I will get there just a few minutes early, maybe that will be a good thing. I don't want to be too early, that would make me seem anxious, and I don't want to get there late – that would just be a bad way to start things out,' she proposed.

Judith could hardly contain her own excitement, 'Yes, now is as good a time as any, you go on over there, and be careful! I will see you at church. Have a great time!' She said as she gave Sierra a reassuring embrace.

Sierra was unusually calm as she made her way to Pastor Will and Mrs. Sabrina's house. The meeting in New Orleans had helped with the awkwardness a little bit. At least they had something more than the weather to talk about this time. Trisha had made sure of that! She was still bubbling inside with the notion of seeing Grayson again, especially now that she knew so much more about him, and truthfully adored every bit.

Sabrina met her at the door as she approached the house. 'Come on in, I was just about to set the table,' she said with a hospitable gesture. As Sierra made her way to the dining room to help with plates, she looked around the house for Grayson. He wasn't in the living room, and he wasn't in the kitchen. Sierra wondered from which direction he would make his entrance.

'Will and Grayson ran down to the store to get some ice and drinks. I had tea made, but Will wanted to get some other drinks just in case you didn't like tea.' Sabrina interjected as if she knew Sierra was wondering where they were. She was kind-of glad to have a few minutes to acclimate herself to the surroundings before the initial 'hello'. She wondered if she should give him a hug when he walked in or just say hi, or what would be the best thing to do since they were at the Pastor's house. She felt sure that her every move was going to be scrutinized as it was clear the Allen's were playing the match-making game.

'Where are the kids?' Sierra asked when she noticed the house to be quieter than she expected. 'They went to the movie with Jarred,' she said. Jarred was their oldest son, he was almost eighteen and about to graduate from high school. Thomas and Richard were younger, probably ten and twelve. Sierra laughed as she considered the fact that the Allen's prearranged for their children to be away for this 'casual' dinner before church. 'What can I do to help,' she said. She wanted something to keep her mind occupied so that she would not watch the door every second for Grayson's arrival.

'Well, I waited until the last minute to put the bread in the oven. If you want to grab that garlic bread out of the freezer I will turn the oven on,' Sabrina directed. About the time she opened the freezer to look for the bread, she heard a car door slam. 'Oh my goodness, he is here, I wonder what he is wearing this time, she thought. Grayson and Will walked through the door with several bags of groceries in their hands. 'I thought you just went to get ice and drinks,' Sabrina chided. 'That's what happens when you send men to the store,' she said as she gave Sierra a reassuring glance. 'We are putting the bread in the oven now. The Lasagna is done, so give us about ten minutes and we will be ready to eat.' she announced.

Grayson looked over at Sierra, winked his eye and said in a flirty voice, 'Sounds like a plan to me!' Sierra just smiled as she watched Grayson pull himself up onto the countertop in the kitchen as if he wanted to watch her get the bread ready. He was wearing a grey, Tennessee sweat suit with a hoodie. He looked so good that she could hardly concentrate.

'Soooo, how was your day,' Sierra said to Grayson as she tried to act natural. 'Well it wasn't half as good as yesterday,' His remark made Sierra blush as she noticed Will and Sabrina's awareness of the chemistry between them. 'Yes, I agree. Yesterday was fun.' she quickly remarked in an effort to fend off their ogles.

As she walked past him on her way to place the bread in the oven, Grayson reached out and pinched her side, 'You look cute,' he bravely remarked. Sierra bashfully replied, 'Thank you, you do too!' She thought about what she said and wondered if it sounded too trite.

'What did you do today?' he queried. Sierra explained to him that her sister-in-law Andrea was expecting and had some complications that morning that landed her in the hospital for a few days. 'They are pretty sure they got it under control, I am going to go by there tomorrow after my job interview,' she explained. 'What job interview,' Grayson replied.

'Oh, I went to a temporary job office at the beginning of the week. There's a big bank in downtown Baton Rouge that has a job opening in the vault. The lady called me today and wants to meet me tomorrow about the position. I think it will be good. She said that it would start out temporary; then become more permanent if I do a good job. So we will see.' She expounded.

'I think that will be good, I will be praying for you to find favor with her in the morning, I am sure you will do fine,' his encouraging words gripped Sierra's heart. She started to feel a touch of that breathlessness that had come over her almost every other time she was in the room with Grayson. 'Um, you are too sweet,' she coyly replied as she looked down at the floor trying to regain her composure. 'Let's go ahead and get some ice in the glasses,' Sabrina instructed. 'Who wants tea?' Will, Grayson, and Sierra responded in unison, 'I do.' With that, Sabrina looked over at Will with a cynical glance and said, 'Boy I sure am glad you went to the store and bought all of those drinks!' 'You're right honey, I guess we didn't need all of those,' he said.

Will whispered to Grayson and Sierra, 'Sometimes it is best just to agree. Trust me on this one.' 'Go on in the dining room and have a seat,' Sabrina said as she pulled the bread out of the oven. 'I will be in as soon as I get this cut up. Sierra if you want to grab a couple of these tea glasses that would be great.'

'Here, let me help you with those,' Grayson said as he reached over and grabbed the other two glasses from the counter-top. As he reached around Sierra for the glasses, she felt the warmth of his body as he stood behind her almost touching her back, and his breath on her neck as he moved in to get his hands on the glasses. She closed her eyes, took a deep breath, and waited for him to step back before she moved a muscle. A she felt her nerves tingle. 'This guy is driving me crazy and he doesn't even know it,' she thought to herself as she picked up on the scent of his cologne again. Sierra did not think Grayson intended to arouse her senses with his attempt to help with the glasses, but wondered if he was aware that he had done just that.

Sabrina finished cutting the bread and they all found their places around the table. 'Let's pray,' Pastor Will said in an effort to get the ball rolling. 'Lord, we come before you today and thank you for the blessings you bestow on our lives. Thank you for this food. Thank you for giving Grayson a safe trip up from New Orleans. Thank you for friends and fellowship. Amen. Let's eat!'

Dinner was like a game of twenty questions. Will and Sabrina were apparently trying to counteract any awkwardness they thought Grayson and Sierra may have been feeling by keeping a steady flow of conversation going throughout the meal. They asked questions of Sierra like, how do you feel about being home from the Air Force, and where did you go to church in Colorado. They asked Grayson when he planned on going back to Tennessee for a visit, and how school was going. Random questions to keep them talking was actually the Allen's way of helping Grayson and Sierra get to know each other a little bit better, but they didn't realize that.

'Thank you for the dinner, Sabrina. It was very good,' Grayson said as he pushed his plate to the side as if he could not eat another bite. 'You are so welcome,' Sabrina came back, 'I am just so glad you and Sierra could be here with us. Church starts in about thirty minutes, so I am going to get in here and clean this kitchen real quick before we have to head over there,' she said as she began grabbing dished. 'Here, let me help you with that,' Sierra said as she too began cleaning off the table. 'Okay then, let's just throw these dishes in the dishwasher. The oven is still warm, let's just cover this bread and lasagna and keep them there until after church. Will and

Grayson may want to eat some more after they get back. 'Will do,' Sierra said.

'If it's alright, I am going to have to get on over to the church and get a few things ready for tonight,' Grayson said. Sierra was positively aware of his polite mannerisms. He always seemed so gentlemanlike and sensitive. 'Sierra, if you want to come in and help me with the youth again tonight – you are more than welcome,' he extended an invitation as he walked to the door. 'Well, as long as you aren't going to wet me down with a water hose I may just be there,' she laughed.

When Grayson was out the door, Sabrina spouted off as if she could not hold her thoughts for one more second. 'Isn't he just the cutest thing? As soon as I heard you were coming home I just knew that you two would hit it off. You know he came in from New Orleans today about two hours earlier than usual. He usually pulls in at the last minute before his youth meeting starts. I think he skipped his afternoon visit to the gym to be here with you. He was so excited. He told us all about your visit in New Orleans yesterday at the River Walk.

'Really,' Sierra said with a surprised look. 'What exactly did he tell you?' she asked. He told us that you looked really cute in your little LSU cap and jeans. He said that he found you with no problem as you were listening to one of the street people play a saxophone by the fountain. He told us about how your friends raked him through the coals with questions, but he was a little disappointed that he didn't learn more about you while he was there. Don't tell him I said so, but I think he hopes to spend a little bit more time with you tonight after church so that he can get to know you better. We told him that you guys are welcome to come back over here after church and sit in the living room. We will not bother you. Actually I think that is why Will bought all of the drinks, and popcorn, and cookies. He is as nervous about this whole ordeal as Grayson is.

'So, you think Grayson is nervous,' Sierra responded. 'Are you kidding me, he is floating around here like he is on cloud nine. You have definitely sparked an interest in him young lady – don't doubt that for a second.' Sabrina said as she wiped off one last counter-top.

'That should just about do it, let me get in here and grab my shoes and we can head on over to the church. You can just leave your car parked in our driveway and we will walk across the field to the church. That will give you an excuse to come back over here when it's over,' Sabrina winked.

Receiving that information caused Sierra to feel confident and anxious at the same time.

'Ok, thank you so much. I really appreciate it. I feel so strange with this 'get to know you' stuff, but it is so evident to me that God is in it that I know it is right. 'I have never been in a situation where Grayson and I were alone in a room together. There has always been an extenuating circumstance, or other activity going on at the same time. The thought of just me and him with no ice-breakers makes me feel butterflies in my stomach,' Sierra admitted to Sabrina.

'Well, that's one reason Will and I thought our place would be perfect. You won't actually be alone. We can all sit in there for a while and chat, eat popcorn or whatever. Then Will and I will go in the other room and watch TV so you guys can talk for a while. We will help you break the ice some, don't worry.' Sabrina was so encouraging and insightful.

'Thank you so much for everything – you will never know how much I appreciate it. By the way, the dinner was great,' Sierra concluded as she broke away from Sabrina to head down the hall to the youth room. 'No problem what-so-ever,' Sabrina replied and walked away. As Sierra opened the door to the youth room, three boys were standing in the middle of the room aiming a water hose straight at her. As soon as she saw them, she turned around and ran down the hall in the other direction. When she did, she ran directly into Grayson who was blocking the exit and laughing.

'So, is this what you had to get over here and set up?' she asked. 'Please, don't get me wet, she begged. I am not in the mood to be soaked,' she pleaded. Grayson reached over and placed his hands on her shoulders. Looking her in the eyes he said, 'Do I look like someone who would do something like that?' 'I don't guess,' she said nervously. 'Okay guys, put it up. She doesn't want to be sprayed with the water hose today,' he taunted as he turned her back around toward the youth room. 'We couldn't turn the hose on inside of the church anyway. I just couldn't resist teasing you since you said you would come as long as we didn't pull out a water hose,' he kidded.

Sierra enjoyed the youth meeting, this time finding her seat on one of the couches as Grayson brought a lesson on purity. It was interesting to her how he came up with such an analogy from the story of Joseph, but he sure did. The kids were in awe of the application to their own lives that he presented, and so was Sierra. He talked to them about how Joseph was a good looking, successful guy who had everything going for him, but he was faced with a choice. At the risk of even death he resisted the advances of Potiphar's wife. As a result he was falsely accused and thrown in to prison.

Grayson brought out the point to the kids that even though Joseph was punished unnecessarily, he was pure before God and that was all that mattered. He explained to them that no matter what temptations come their way, no matter what rumors are spread, what is important is that they are pure before the Lord. Using the Scripture reference from Mark 4:22; Grayson explained to the youth that whatever is done in secret will be brought out into the light eventually. He made it clear that even the things that are done uprightly in times when no one is looking will be a reward to them in the future. He explained to them that no one would have been there to see Joseph if he had given in to Potiphar's wife. She wouldn't have tried to ruin him, and he would have gone on as the King's right-hand man gaining riches and popularity along the way. But Joseph knew that no matter what everyone else could see, God was watching.

Sierra knew that Grayson's message was directed toward the teenagers and the peer pressures they face, but she heard the Lord speak deeply into her spirit while he presented the truths of integrity from God's word. She wanted to be that type of person. She wanted to be pure before God.

Chapter Fourteen

After the message and a time of refreshments with the youth, Grayson approached Sierra. 'I was wondering if you have a little bit of time after we are done here to chat. I would like to get to know you a little bit better,' he admitted to her with a nervous grin.

'Actually, I left my car parked at the Allen's house. Sabrina invited me to come over for a little while after church, so that would work out fine,' she answered in reply to his invitation. Great, let me just wind things up around here and we will walk over with Brother Will and Sabrina, he concluded. 'I will go to the sanctuary and let my mom know what I am doing so she won't worry,' Sierra said with enthusiasm. Sierra nearly tripped over a chair as she turned to head for the sanctuary, and hoped Grayson hadn't noticed.

The service had let out only seconds before Sierra made it to the back door of the sanctuary. People greeted her as she held the door for them to exit. She knew her mom would still be there. She always sits at the organ and waits for everyone else before she makes her way to the exit. 'Hey mom, Brother Allen and Sabrina invited me to come back over to their house for a while after church, so I will be home later,' she informed Judith. 'I guess things went well over dinner,' Judith supposed.

Sierra explained that the Allen's had asked a million questions and it gave them an opportunity to get to know each other a little bit better. She told her about the water-hose episode, and said he had mentioned to her that he would like to get to know her better.

'I am really excited, but feel a little bit vulnerable at the same time,' she confessed.

'Something would be wrong if you didn't feel that way. Ok – have fun. I am so happy things are working out with Grayson. I just knew there was something about him that you would connect with,' her mother proudly admitted.

Sierra headed back to the fellowship hall to wait for Grayson to finish straightening up from the youth's refreshment time. About the time he finished folding the last table, Pastor Allen walked through the fellowship hall and said, 'Ya'll ready – the popcorn is waiting!' 'Yep, answered Grayson, let me just grab my Bible.'

Sabrina was in the parking lot waiting for them to come out. The four of them reflected on the happenings of the night as they laughed and walked toward the Allen's home. 'I heard you almost got hosed down tonight Sierra,' Pastor Allen joked. 'I really think they would have done it if I had not been inside of the church,' Sierra disclosed. 'Well, we almost went for it,' Grayson confessed, but when I saw the look on your face when you were begging for mercy I gave the boys the symbol to 'cut.' 'I didn't think that would be a very positive start to the evening, especially when I wanted to talk to you after church,' he divulged.

'Thank you for changing your mind,' she retorted. Having grown up with three brothers, she was familiar with the practical jokes guys could play, but she would have to admit she was a little surprised that Grayson was already playing such games with her. 'The youth asked me if you were coming tonight,' he explained. When I told them what you said about 'if there is not a water hose pointed at you' they got the bright idea to go get the hose. 'I have to admit, I went along with it, but it was honestly not my idea,' he justified.

Will and Sabrina laughed with delight as they listened to Grayson and Sierra's discussion. They were happy to be a part of their new-found rapport. 'I bought some of that caramel popcorn when we went to the store earlier, Sabrina you can't have any since you didn't think we needed it,' he said with a sarcastic tone. 'I got some cookies and drinks too. I thought everyone might want a little snack,' he clarified with a smile as he rolled his eyes over in Sabrina's direction.

'I am still stuffed from that lasagna,' Sierra immediately responded. 'Grayson over there doesn't eat a lot of sweets in case you couldn't tell, so I didn't really buy the good stuff for him. You are going to have to eat some of it or Sabrina will be on my case for sure,' Will begged.

'You don't eat popcorn,' Sierra asked with a puzzled look. 'Well, with my workout regime I have conditioned myself to a strict diet. I don't eat a lot of sweets, fried food, and soft drinks. They are really terrible for you anyway, so I just got out of the habit of eating junk food when I was competing and I have never got back into it,' Grayson elucidated.

'Well what in the world do you eat?' Sierra asked. I eat rice, vegetables, meats that aren't fried, fruits, and I mostly drink water. After a workout I will go for pizza or something high in carbs, and I usually eat a pack of noodles or something like that at night so my muscles will respond to the morning workout. It is just what you get used to I guess,' he explained as she glared at him with a strange look on her face. Sierra had never met anyone who was that disciplined with their diet and exercise schedule. In the service she had to do PT, and run, but that was as far as it went.

'So I guess going to get hot donuts at midnight is out of the question for someone like you,' she laughed. She and her friends would often do just that. The donut place in downtown Baton Rouge was open twenty-four hours a day, and they have hot donuts every hour. It was one of Sierra's favorite things to do. 'Well, of course I would go,' he said. 'I don't think I would actually eat a donut, unless it was an apple filled one, but I would go,' he admitted.

'He's just a weirdo; we don't let him bother us. Honey, pop some of that caramel popcorn, and I will put the cookies in the oven and pour us some drinks. Grayson, you can get a bottle of water, you know where to find it. See, Sierra, you just have to be yourself and don't let all of that diet talk intimidate you, Brother Allen said as he patted his belly and laughed.

'Ha, okay thanks for the heads-up!' Sierra said lightheartedly as she grabbed the pack of cookies and began placing them on the cookie sheet. Sabrina pulled a game out of the closet, she thought that would be a great way to keep everyone engaged in an activity so they could avoid any times of awkward silence. 'We love to play board games,' she admitted. 'With everyone's busy schedule it is often difficult to spend quality time together. Once in a while it is great to just stop everything, turn off the television, and play a good game,' Sabrina contended.

'Will, come over here and explain the rules to the game,' she commanded. It was a game using chips and cards that a friend of theirs had apparently made for them, so Sierra had never seen it before, but it was pretty easy to learn. 'Sounds fun,' Grayson said. 'Now – we will have to divide up into teams. Do you want to play guys against girls, or do ya'll wanna play against us?' Will asked as he pulled the colored chips out of a bag. 'Well, since Sierra and I have never played before - we would be at a terrible disadvantage if we played against two pros like yourselves, so for at least the first round I think we should play girls against guys,' Grayson stipulated. 'The first team to get five in a row - twice wins. That's about the sum of it. You lay chips on cards and try to get five in a row without being blocked by the other team.'

'Well that sounds pretty easy, let's go for it,' Grayson replied. 'Okay then Gray-man, don't make me look bad,' Will prodded Grayson with his elbow. The Allens played two rounds of the game with Grayson and Sierra before they decided it was getting late and they were going to go on in their room and watch television before they went to bed. Sierra was relieved that the ice had been broken, but felt a nervous flood pour over her at the thought of being there for the first time all alone with Grayson.

'Do you mind leaving the game out – Grayson and I may want to play one more round before I have to go home,' Sierra said hoping they would agree. She thought that would be a wonderful way to keep from the one-on-one weirdness of just the two of them trying to come up with a good thing to talk about. 'That will be fine,' Sabrina said. 'Don't even worry about putting it up, I will do that in the morning. Ya'll just have fun with it. Goodnight.' With that, Sabrina and Will disappeared behind the door of the hallway and pulled it shut. Sierra was really glad that they pulled the door shut, she was paranoid that they would be watching behind the cracked opening otherwise. 'I am just being paranoid,' she thought to herself as she grabbed the green chips and pushed the red ones over in Grayson's direction.

As she got the bag of red chips to Grayson's side of the table, he put his hand on hers as if to stop her in her tracks. 'Look at me,' he said in a little above a whisper. Sierra felt sure Grayson could hear her heart pounding, as she could barely hear anything else. She felt her cheeks fill with blood, and it was suddenly very hot at that table.

Grayson had been a 'take charge' kind of guy with his youth group. He knew how to get out of them what he wanted. Apparently he had the same power over Sierra. She looked into his piercing eyes and felt as if he could see through to her soul. At that moment, without letting go of her hand, he began to speak as if he had rehearsed his lines all day long.

'I know it is as obvious to you as it is to me that something miraculous is taking place between us,' he opened. 'The moment you walked into that fellowship hall Sunday morning, I felt a change in my life that I have never felt before, and do not expect I will ever feel again,' he said while never wavering from his piercing glare into her eyes.

'Sierra Bradley, I am not sure what your life story was about before this week, but I believe I can say with certainty that you and I have activated a new volume in that series. I am not sure what it is that God is doing, but I know beyond a shadow of a doubt that he wants to accomplish something in my life and he wants to use you to do it,' he went on. 'I hope I am not scaring you, but God has a way of making His will clear to me so that I don't have a choice but to follow it. It is black and white. And since Sunday I have done nothing but pray and seek the Lord about whatever it is that is going on inside of me concerning you,' he explained.

'I feel that the Lord wants me to tell you this from Isaiah 55: 8, For my thoughts are not your thoughts, neither are my ways your ways, declares the Lord,' Grayson quoted the scripture before explaining himself. 'See Sierra, I believe God knows that we are flabbergasted by the whirlwind he has thrown us into over the past few days. In men's eyes it makes no sense that I would even be sitting here right now telling you these things, but here I am.' He said with a beautiful smile.

'Sunday night when I came to the window of your mom's vehicle and told you that message God had given me for you about any windows in your life being opened - well, all the way back to New Orleans I pondered those words in my heart. I asked God why he would want me to tell you that, and why I was feeling like I had met you for a reason,' he reflected.

'The funny thing is; God didn't give me an answer. All I know is that the only thing I could think of on Monday was you. When Brother Allen called and told me you were going to be in New Orleans on Tuesday, I wanted to drop everything I was doing and go find you right then. I actually did skip my noon class and go down to the River Walk yearning to run into you somewhere. Then, when I saw you by that fountain, I think my heart literally skipped a beat. That is why I was so eager to answer the questions your friends posed to me even though they were quite personal, I feel like that meeting was ordained by God. He wanted you to learn about me, and tonight I am here with you because I think he wants me to learn more about you.'

Sierra was astounded by his articulate display of feelings that mirrored her own. She felt numb and speechless, humbled and overwhelmed. 'Well, what do you want to know,' she said as she pulled her hand back to her lap. 'Everything, Sierra, I want to know everything. What is your middle name? What is your favorite color? Why did you join the Air Force? What is your hobby? What are you good at - and not so good at?' Grayson began listing out questions he wanted answers to regarding Sierra Bradley's life.

'Well, my middle name is Nicole, but I don't tell that to just anyone, so feel honored,' she began in an effort to answer his questions. 'So, what is your middle name,' she retaliated. 'Ha, I guess I deserve that. My middle name is Kyle. Grayson Kyle Raines; is that better,' he smiled. As Sierra began to talk, Grayson sat back in his chair with the most fascinated look on his face, and listened intently. My favorite color is purple. I joined the Air Force because I did not want to stay home with my parents while I went to college, and since I didn't get scholarships to pay for my school, the military seemed like a reasonable route to take. Now I am not so sure I would do that again, but the experience was good, and I have money to go to school now when I get ready. Hmmm, my hobby, that's a good question, I am not sure what my hobby is, she said as she attempted to look Grayson in the eyes for a second. She could not keep her focus on him for very long because his gaze was so deep it was almost intimidating to her. Sierra had lived a life so far removed from who she truly was in her heart for so long that the things she would have considered hobbies a week ago were no longer even remotely interesting.

'I am exploring my interest right now, I don't know what my hobbies are,' she admitted to Grayson. I guess you could say I am good at singing. I am pretty good at writing, and I am learning to cook. 'Anything else?' she said laughingly.

Grayson did not waver; his serious tone revealed the genuine intent of his heart, to learn more about the girl God had put in his path. 'If you could change one thing about your life, what would it be?' He asked. 'Oh my goodness,' Sierra thought as she pondered that question in her heart. 'He is psycho-analyzing me. He wants to see if I am crazy or something.' 'Are you psycho-analyzing me?' Sierra asked with a grin, having learned earlier that Grayson earned his undergraduate degree in psychology, and had worked in a Psych ward during his last year of college. 'No, not really,' he said with a smile. 'I just want to find out more about you and the best way to get you to talk is to ask questions. You will be more prone to answer if I break my questions down into smaller segments of thought.' he explained.

'So, he IS psycho-analyzing me, great!' she thought, but decided to go with it anyway. What would I change if I could choose one thing? 'Hmmm' –she thought as she pondered the best response for one who was analyzing her every word. 'Now I could go overboard here and tell him about all of the days in my life that were – well – less than perfect, or I can use this as an opportunity to show him how far I have come,' She decided to go with the latter of the two choices.

'Well, Grayson, everybody has things that go on in their lives that they would have chosen to avoid if given the opportunity. However, those things are what make us who we are. Although there are situations that I would not want to even consider living through again, I would not change them for any amount of money because I am who I am today, I view the world from the perspective that I do, and I focus on the future with regard to those life lessons I have been taught as a result of both lovely - and unlovely situations along the way. I have not always recognized that God was in control of every situation in my life for the purpose of getting me to a point that He could use me for his good, but I do now. Even if only this week, I understand that everything that happens... happens for a reason. Because of that, I have to answer your question with one word...nothing, I wouldn't change a single thing about my life, even if I could,' Sierra responded genuinely from her heart.

Grayson appeared mesmerized, 'Thank you so much Sierra for sharing your heart with me, I am breathless. That was definitely not the answer I expected to hear, but I must admit it is the best one you could have given!' He replied.

Chapter Fifteen

'Are there any other pressing questions you would like to ask me,' Sierra welcomed the possibility that he did, even though it was getting pretty late and she had that job interview the next morning. 'Do you have an early class in the morning?' She asked. 'Well, not too early. My first class isn't until 10 o'clock tomorrow, so I have a little bit of freedom. I will probably stay here tonight and drive to New Orleans in the morning. I would hate to fall asleep on the way there tonight,' he laughed.

'Just a couple more questions. First, do you have a picture of yourself that I can have? I have told just about everyone at the seminary about you and they want to see your picture.' Sierra was honored, yet amazed that Grayson had already told all of his friends about her. 'Well, I guess it is no different than me telling everyone in my life about him. Boy, he must really be feeling the same thing I feel. I can't believe it!' she thought to herself. 'I will have to get you one out of my car when I go out, I didn't bring my purse in,' she said through a blushing grin.

'Ok, one more thing,' Grayson voiced as he grabbed hold of her wrist softly and pulled her back down into her seat. 'I am going home to Tennessee next week for my cousin's wedding. If you would be willing to go with me, I would be honored. I would love for you to meet my mom and dad. They just have to meet you and this would be a perfect opportunity,' he said with hopeful air. Sierra was taken aback by the invitation to meet Grayson's family already. PJ had been avoiding that situation for nearly two years, and now after just a few days he says his parents *have* to meet me. 'Whew!' she thought. It was almost overwhelming, but she just knew; in the deepest part of her soul, that it was right.

'I have that job interview in the morning. Let me talk to that Lucille lady and tell her that I can start this week, but next week I will not be available because I already have plans. If she agrees to let me do that, I would be honored to go and meet your family,' she nervously replied.

'Before we go get that picture, I just want to tell you how thankful I am that you were willing to listen to the Lord tonight and obey Him. If you feel even half as overwhelmed as I do by this whole situation, I know that it would have been the easier thing to just run away from me for fear of saying the wrong thing. But you didn't do that. You made this relationship transition so much easier for me to accept as reality. I don't know why at this particular time in our lives God chose to make our paths meet, but I can tell you that I am thankful He did, and no matter what comes out of it, I will never – ever be the same person I was a week ago,' she humbly disclosed.

'Let's go get that picture so you can head home. It is almost twelve-thirty. The morning will be here before we know it, he encouraged. Sierra and Grayson headed out the garage door to where Sierra had parked her car. She opened her glove box to get a picture of herself. She had a stack of wallet sized photos that were part of a set she had made a few months back and never got around to sending out. 'Here you go, it isn't the best, but it's me,' she said as she handed him the photo. Grayson held the picture into the light of her car so that he could get a good look at it. 'Thank you. Thank you so much. This is beautiful – and I am not just saying that either. You are really a beautiful girl. Your brown hair and green eyes look really amazing with the pink dress you are wearing,' he remarked as he intently studied the picture.

'Now, can I ask you one last question,' Sierra pressed as she waited for him to put the photo down. 'What kind of cologne do you wear because that is all I have been able to think about since Sunday,' she admitted. 'I think it is called *Fine*. My mom gave it to me before I left to move to New Orleans, I will have to check the bottle and see exactly what it is. I am glad you like it. Knowing that, I will make sure I wear it every day!' He said with a wink. Sierra thought *Fine* was the perfect name for Grayson's cologne for more reasons than one.

'Now, before you go, do you mind if I just give you a hug,' he said. 'Man, a hug,' Sierra thought. She was sure hoping he was going to ask for a kiss before she left, but a hug would be better than nothing. It was actually amazing to her that he respected her enough to not push a kiss on her, and that he even asked for a hug. 'Wow,' she sighed.

Sierra felt like she would melt as Grayson pulled her in close to his chest and wrapped his strapping arms around her. It was obvious to her that he did not intend to let go quickly, so she just rested her head against his chest and thanked God for blessing her beyond her wildest imagination. She closed her eyes and took in the moment, hoping it would be the first of many in the days and years to come.

After what seemed like ten minutes, Grayson loosened his grip. As Sierra lifted her head from his chest, he placed his hands on the sides of her head and kissed her forehead tenderly. 'Goodnight,' he whispered as he observably resisted the urge to kiss her lips. 'I will be praying for you tomorrow as you go for your job interview,' he said as he stepped away so she could walk around and get in her car.

Sierra felt light on her feet, she had a time walking to the driver's side of the car. 'I guess this is what it feels like to be swept off of your feet,' she actually said out loud to Grayson. He laughed and said, 'I hope you are right, Sierra, I hope you are right.' Sierra quietly said goodnight as she sat down in her car. She rolled down the passenger side window and told Grayson that she hoped he had a safe trip back to New Orleans in the morning and a wonderful rest of the week.

'I will call you if I can,' Grayson said, 'but on a youth pastor salary I will have to make the calls short,' he laughed. Sierra waved and backed out of the driveway. 'But I will be back up on Saturday before noon. The youth have a car-wash if you want to come you are welcome. I can swing by your dad and mom's house and pick you up around ten o'clock. 'Okay, that sounds like a plan,' she said then she reminded him that she would find out the next day about that trip to Tennessee.

At the end of the Allen's long driveway, Sierra stopped long enough to get her breath. It was all she could do to hold back the tears. She was certainly not sad, so crying seemed a bit strange to her. She had heard of people being 'so happy they could cry,' but it had never happened to her until that moment.

As she drove home, she tried to sort out all of the emotions that were running through her head but it was no use. She just gave into them and cried the happiest cry of her life.

Chapter Sixteen

'I will just take a shower in the morning,' she thought as she walked into the house and headed to the back bedroom. She wondered if she could make herself go to sleep with all of the hype she was feeling. Her adrenaline was at an all-time high. She felt like she could run to the moon and back, but she needed to get to sleep. Tomorrow was going to be a full day.

Sierra tossed and turned for a while, trying to settle down. She prayed thanking God for what he was doing in her life – even though she could not try to explain it. The next thing she knew, the alarm clock was buzzing. It was time to get up. Sierra felt like she had only been in the bed for a few minutes.

She walked into the kitchen where Judith was fixing breakfast for Stan. 'Up and at-um, you have a long day ahead of you,' she said. 'Yeah, I am going to go by and get something for Andrea before I go to the hospital. Are you sure you don't want to go with me? I could drop you off at the mall or something while I go for the interview,' she suggested.

'Well you know, I was headed to the hospital today anyway, so I guess that could work out perfectly,' she decided. 'Will you have time to do that? I wouldn't want you to be late for your interview,' she insisted. 'Right now it is only seven-thirty. I don't have to be there until ten," she said positively. 'Ok; well, let me get your dad off to work and I will get ready and go with you. That will be more fun anyway,' Judith insisted.

Sierra was glad her mom was going to go with her. She could hardly wait to tell her about what happened last night. Sierra grabbed a box of cereal as she thought about what she should wear for the interview. 'Should I wear a dress or pants today?' she asked Judith. Without having to think about it Judith responded, 'I think what you wore to the job office was perfect. Why don't you just wear that again? You will not be over dressed – and you will not be underdressed in that outfit. That looks like something a person working at a bank would wear anyway.' 'That's a good idea. I will just go with that, Sierra agreed.

Stan walked in the kitchen on his way out the door to work. 'Good luck with your interview today – man, what time did you get home? We waited up for you as long as we could, then we had to call it a night.' He harassed dramatically. 'What in the world were ya'll doing at the Preacher's house till midnight? I didn't think anything exciting went on over there,' he laughed.

'Sabrina has a game that one of her friends made for her. We were playing that game. We made cookies and popcorn, and then we just talked. It was fun,' she recapped. 'So Grainey was glad you were there, huh?' Stan remarked. Sierra laughed at her dad and told him that he seemed to be very glad she was there. 'Are you sure you want to get all mixed up with a preacher type?' He asked with a serious tone in his voice, and a joking look of his face. 'You know what they say about those preacher boys...' he laughed. 'No, daddy, I don't know. What do 'they' say about those preacher boys?' she asked. 'You've just gotta watch out for um' that's all,' Stan winked, patted Sierra on the back, grabbed his lunch box, and headed out the door saying, 'You girls have a great day and tell Andrea I am thinking about her.'

'He is so funny. How does he come up with some of the stuff he says,' Sierra asked with a chuckle. 'That's just Stan,' Judith replied. 'When God made him, He broke the mold.'

'Okay, let's hurry up and get ready. I want to hear about how your visit with Grayson went.' Judith said with haste.

As the grandfather clock struck nine o'clock, Judith and Sierra were walking out the door. 'So, start from the beginning, how was the dinner?' Judith asked with anticipation.

'I was so nervous, but when I got to the Allen's house, Grayson was not there. He had gone with Pastor Allen to the grocery store to get ice. Because of that, I had a minute to prepare myself and I felt a bit more at ease. When they finally walked in, Pastor Allen was really good about breaking the ice. He had bags and bags of drinks and snacks. It was funny because Sabrina told him not to get all of that stuff and he got it anyway.' She began.

'Grayson finally came in and plopped himself right up on the countertop and watched everything I was doing to help Sabrina get the food ready. He was flirting. He told me I looked cute, and stood all close to me when we were getting the glasses to put on the table. I was having a hard time catching my breath!' she laughed.

'We had lasagna. It was pretty good. Grayson went on over to the church to get ready for the youth and I helped Sabrina clean up the kitchen. Afterward, Sabrina suggested I keep my car parked at their house and stay a while after church. So, we walked over. When I got to the youth room, some boys were aiming a water hose at me. I turned to run and Grayson was blocking my way. See, I told Grayson that if he promised not to shoot me down with a water hose I would go in with the youth again that night. He was playing a practical joke on me. I really believe if we had not been inside of the church building he would have allowed them to spray me.

Anyway, he preached a marvelous message on purity from the story of Joseph. I guess it has been a while since I have been in church listening to messages, so maybe anything would have seemed good to me, but I am telling you he brought things out of that story with Potiphar's wife that I had never even considered would apply to teenagers and the peer pressures they face.

I really enjoyed it.

After church was over and I came in and talked to you for a minute, then we walked back over to the Allen's house. They joked around with me because they had heard about the water hose stunt Grayson pulled. He defended himself saying that it was the teenager's idea. I was just glad I didn't actually get wet.

We got to the house, and I found out that Grayson is on a strict diet with his work out plan. We made cookies and popcorn and had all kinds of drinks, but he didn't eat any of it. He drank water the whole night! I told him it was too bad he didn't like to go get hot donuts at midnight because that was one of my favorite things to do. He laughed and said he would go if they had an apple filled donut.

Sierra had a neat game for us to play. It was some kind of board with cards on it that you divide up into teams and try to get five in a row —twice. We played a couple of times before the Allen's went on to bed. Grayson and I were going to play a round of the game by ourselves before I went home, but when they went to bed – he started to talk earnestly to me. He put his hand on mine and would not let it go.

'What did he talk to you about?' Judith inquired with intensity. 'It was really amazing, it was like he opened my heart and stole the feelings and thoughts right out of my very being. He is a 'cut to the chase' kind of guy, that's for sure. He basically said that it was obvious to both of us that something was happening between us and he had prayed about it all week. He said that God deals with him very directly, and when the 'writing is on the wall' it is hard for him to ignore it,' she went on.

'I guess you are his 'writing on the wall,' this time huh,' Judith said with a confident glow. 'I guess so! He said that he was preoccupied with thoughts of me all day on Monday. When he found out that I was going to be in New Orleans on Tuesday he skipped his second class to go to the River Walk and look for me. He said he was itching to see me. He said that he was open with Rachael and Trisha because he felt that God wanted me to learn more about him, and he had invited me to stay after church so that he could learn more about me.

'Wow! What did you tell him?' she asked. 'At first I just listened. He was so passionate with his words that it sounded almost like a rehearsed speech. He said he wanted to know everything about me. He started asking questions and I tried to answer them the best way I could. I'm telling you, it was a real soul searching time for me and Grayson didn't even realize it. He asked some simple questions like -what was my favorite color, and why I joined the Air Force. But then he asked me a question I didn't quite know how to answer,' Sierra admitted.

'What was it?' Judith could not contain her eagerness to know more as she gripped the edge of her seat with anticipation of Sierra's answer. She went on, 'You know he has a degree in Psychology. Well I felt like he was reaching deep into my soul to dig out something that would not normally surface. I felt like he was trying to get me to reveal any secrets I may have so that we could deal with them right then and there. He said, 'If you could change one thing about your life what would it be?'

'I felt vulnerable enough to just tell him my entire life story without hesitation. You know more than anyone that I would never even consider doing such a thing with anyone else in the world. I wanted to, but...I didn't. I thought about all of the things that happened when I was fifteen, and about the struggles I faced later being a woman in the military, but I did not spout off with an answer right away. I tried to use wisdom and discernment to let him know that although bad things happen sometimes, how we view those things will determine their outcome. I told him that I could tell him some sob-stories, but I that I felt it was more important for him to know who I am now, and how far I have come rather than all the dirt. I almost felt like he already knew some of it and wanted to get my version of what he had already heard,' she explained.

'Mom, you will never know how much the words you spoke to me after that incident transformed my way of thinking, and my whole outlook on life. You are the reason I can be an overcomer in any situation life throws my way,' she disclosed. 'What did I say,' Judith asked as she pondered that conversation in her mind. 'You told me that I could look at my situation from two different angles.

I could either take a, 'why me' approach to the whole ordeal, or I could realize that this had happened, today was a new day, and I could move on knowing that 'no weapon formed against me shall prosper.' You used the example of a family whose house burned down. You painted a picture for me of the ruins, and the sense of loss they would feel at having everything they had worked for go up in flames,' she reminded Judith of her words.

You said, 'No matter what that family does, there is nothing they can do to recover or replace most of what they lost in the fire. They have to pick themselves up, move past it and start over. They have each other, and they have learned that is all that really matters when it is all said and done. You told me that I had experienced a similar loss in my own life, and what had been 'burned' would never be the same, but today is a new day and I can face it with confidence because I am here, I am alive, and the enemy did not win!'

The trials I faced in the Air Force could have been the 'straw that broke the camel's back.' I always thought lightening didn't strike twice in the same place, but I was strong because those same words resonated within my very being. I truly am an overcomer and it is largely because of you. So – thank you mom. If I never told you that before, I am telling you know. Thank you!'

Sierra said as she looked over at Judith who had a tear rolling down her cheek.

'I love you honey, you know that,' Judith said while trying not to choke-up. 'So, if you didn't tell him the dirt, what did you tell him?' She asked. "I told him that I would not change a thing about my life, even if I could, because the experiences I have had, both good and bad, have worked together to make me the person I am today. I told him that everybody alive has things that they would rather not have lived through – but those things should make, not break a person.'

'I am so proud of you. You are wise beyond your years my dear,' Judith said in admiration. 'So then what happened?' She pressed for the story to continue. Well, he was floored by answer to that question. It was almost as if he didn't know how to respond.

117

'He said that I could not have given a better answer. Then he asked me for a picture. He said that he had told everyone he knew at the seminary about me and he wanted to show them a picture.' 'I actually had a few pictures in my car left over from the ones I had made at the beginning of the year, so I told him I would give him one when we went out to the car before I left,' she explained.

'His last question was surely unexpected if I do say so myself, but welcome nonetheless,' Sierra said while attempting to hold back a smile. 'What? What did he ask you?' Judith blurted out. 'He said that he has to go to Tennessee next week for his cousin's wedding. He said that his parents just *have* to meet me, and that he would feel honored if I would go with him! Can you believe that? He is asking me to come meet his family. PJ avoided that situation like the plague. I am not used to this. What if they don't like me? I am going to ask the lady at the job interview if I can start the following week so that I can go. If she agrees, then I will have my answer!' Sierra said with a giddy look.

'Then, he asked if he could hug me. Can you believe that? He actually said, 'Do you mind if I give you a hug!' I was thinking, 'Do I mind...I was hoping for more than that.' He was such a gentleman. He pulled me to his chest and held me there for a long time, brushing my hair with his hand. I could hear his heart pounding as I rested my head against him. I could smell his cologne, and I even asked him what kind it was. Ha! He said knowing I like it he will wear it every day!

Anyway, when he stopped hugging me, he reached out and put his hands on the sides of my head and kissed my forehead real sweet. I felt like I was going to pass right out! Literally, I could barely walk around the car to drive home. I rolled down the window on my way out and he invited me to the youth car wash on Saturday. He said he would pick me up around ten that morning. He may call before then, but I don't really expect him to.

'Goodness Sierra, it sounds like we need to go dress shopping - and I don't mean to wear to church on Sunday!' Judith said in reply to Sierra's awe inspiring story. 'Hey, that would be fun. Why don't we do it just for the fun of it after I get finished at the bank?' Sierra was delighted with the idea. 'I wish Andrea could go with us, she used to work at that Bridal Boutique across town. She would know the good ones to try on. Well, we will just go have fun with it, why not?' Judith seemed more excited about the whole situation than Sierra was.

'Do you just want me to drop you off at the mall while I go downtown, or do you want to walk around the Capital building instead? I don't expect this to take very long. Today is just an initial interview, I won't start the job today,' Sierra asked. 'Actually, it is a beautiful day to walk around the Capital grounds, I think that will be a great idea, and anyway it is really close to the bank. You can just park in one spot and I will meet you back at the car when you are done,' Judith agreed.

The Louisiana State Capital was known for its beautiful gardens, and scenic overlook onto the Mississippi River. Sierra remembered going there on field trips when she was a kid in school. She loved the rolling hills, and the big cannon that sat on top of the highest one. She remembered a bell that always reminded her of the liberty bell that sat at the bottom of one of the hills. The building itself is thirty-four stories high. She remembered how scared she would be when they rode the elevator to the top and looked out over the city from the viewing area with the wind blowing in her hair. The whole area was like an escape from reality. The horse-drawn carriages gave the whole area a 'take you back in time' feeling.

'Ok mom, I will park right here. Just keep an eye on the car periodically, and when I get finished, that's where I will be waiting for you. Have fun!" she said as she put a few quarters into the parking meter on the curb. As Sierra turned to face the bank towers, she was surprisingly confident. 'Lucille Watson, here I come,' she said aloud with a snicker as she made her way to the entrance.

'My name is Sierra Bradley. I am here for a meeting with Lucille Watson. She told me to check in at the front desk and I would be directed to the appropriate office,' Sierra said as she attempted to sound professional. 'Yes, Mrs. Bradley, right this way. Lucille is expecting you.' The older lady in a pink over-coat said as she took off down the corridor gesturing Sierra to follow. The walked to the elevator, and went down one floor. In such a tall building, Sierra half expected to go up, but if she was going to work in the vault, it made perfect sense to go down instead.

'If you will have a seat in this waiting area, I will let Mrs. Watson know that you are here,' the lady spoke in a sweet voice. Sierra sat upright and crossed her legs as not to appear slouchy. After about five minutes, a distinguished black woman, apparently in her late thirties, walked out of the office with a beautiful smile, moved toward Sierra with her had held out, and said, 'Hello, you must be Miss Bradley. I am Lucille Watson and I am so glad you are here today. If you will step right into my office, I would love to talk with you.'

'It is very nice to meet you too,' Sierra replied as she stood, shook Mrs. Watson's hand, and walked into her office. 'Have a seat, make yourself comfortable. Can I get you anything to drink?' Lucille said in an effort to relieve any tension Sierra may have felt. 'No – thank you. I am fine,' Sierra replied with quiet poise.

'Judging from your profile from the job agency, you are more than qualified for the position we are attempting to fill. I was actually excited to see that you are multi-talented,' Lucille started off the interview with complimentary words that made Sierra feel some of the pressure relieved. 'We went through the agency because we knew they would narrow the choices for us better than we could adequately do it ourselves. For that reason, the job is listed with the agency as a temporary, two week position. However, in the event that you are able to do the job as well as we anticipate, the opportunity will be available for you to become an employee of the bank directly, rather than a temp,' she divulged.

'What exactly does the job entail?' Sierra asked. 'I was just about to get into that, so I am glad you asked. We have a huge vault on this floor. I will take you there in a few minutes. Important records are kept there, such as deeds to properties, inheritance entitlements, titles, wills, and such. Often individuals, family members, lawyer's offices and such will check out the documents for various reasons. Authorized individuals only can take the actual documents, and they must sign a form before doing so. Other individuals who are listed as having access only to the files can sign to have a copy of a document in the vault, but are not permitted to take the original. Your job would be to monitor those requests, and keep those records. You would also be expected to re-file all of the removed documents at the end of each business day in the proper place. You have a copy machine that will be used to photocopy documents for authorized customers, and a logbook for the date, time, and specific document that was photocopied, then the authorized taker will sign for the copy. It is a very organized system because many of these are sensitive, legal documents that could really cause a problem if handled improperly.

And that is about it," Lucille explained. 'We have three other employees who work in this office area, so you will not be down here alone. You will, however be the only one authorized to sign out documents or copies of documents. This alleviates the possibility that a document of high priority would go missing,' she expressed.

'So, if you don't have any questions about that, we can head on back to my office and talk a little bit more about the details,' Lucille guided. Sierra followed Lucille to the office while she rehearsed in her mind how she would ask Lucille about the possibility of starting the job after the trip to Tennessee that she so wanted to make with Grayson.

As Lucille sat back down behind her desk she said, 'Now, the job itself will not actually start until a week from Monday. The last employee left the vault in much disarray. We have two of our people who are familiar with the vault working diligently to get things back in order, but it is going to take them some time. So, if you can start with us a week from Monday, everything should be in perfect order. Our expectation is that you will work to keep it that way. If we are pleased with your performance after the first two weeks, I will meet back with you about the transition from the temporary office to becoming a permanent employee with benefits and the whole ball of wax. Does that sound good?" Lucille asked.

'Yes, actually that sounds great,' Sierra responded in an attempt to hamper her excitement. 'Okay then, we will see you in about ten days. Thank you for coming!' Lucille said as she reached out to shake Sierra's hand one last time.

As Sierra walked back through the corridor, she had a skip in her step. She got a job in a bank that would probably become permanent with benefits, and it doesn't start until after the trip to Tennessee with Grayson. 'How perfect is that,' she shouted as she ran across the street to her car.

She didn't see Judith anywhere, so she found a cast-iron bench near her parking spot and took a seat figuring she would show up before long. 'We could go find a gift for Andrea, stop by the hospital for a while. Then, we can go get some lunch and do the dress thing before we go home. That should be fun,' she thought as she waited for her mom.

'Hey mom!' She shouted as she saw Judith across the field from where she was sitting. 'Hey, how did it go?' Judith said as she made her way towards the car. 'It went really well. Are you ready to go, or do you still want to look around?' Sierra asked in an effort not to rush her. 'Oh, you know how it is, you could stay here all day and get lost in the serenity of the place, but all good things must come to an end. Anyway, we need to get on down to the hospital if we are going to go play dress-up. I don't want to be gone when your daddy gets home from work.' She replied. Sierra told her all about the job interview, the perfect timing of the start date, the possibility of the temporary position becoming permanent, and about the benefits. 'I don't think things can get any better than they are at this very moment of my life,' Sierra said as she drove toward the hospital.

'I am so excited for you. It seems like you are just right where God wants you to be, and He is just opening those windows of heaven and pouring out blessings all over you girl.' Judith bubbled.

Chapter Seventeen

'The hospital where Andrea is staying has an amazing gift shop. I know we can go somewhere else and try to find her something, but I am not going to lie, I would go to that hospital gift shop and buy a gift even if it was not for someone in the hospital. It is not your normal gift shop,' Judith insisted. 'Okay then, let's just do that, then they can deliver it to the room or we can carry it in, either one,' Sierra agreed.

Sierra and Judith walked around the gift shop looking at all of the beautiful gifts. 'You were right when you said this is no ordinary gift shop,' Sierra said. 'I just love this little pink bear – but as soon as we got it she would find out she is having a boy.' 'Yeah, I think we should go with something more neutral to be on the safe side,' her mom agreed. They looked at turtles, and giraffes, brown teddy bears, and monkeys, but they both knew their search was over when Sierra found a huge, white, fluffy elephant with a green bow tied around its neck. "This is it!" Sierra said gleefully. "I don't have to look any farther. I love it!" She exclaimed. 'Perfect,' Judith resounded, 'Now let's just get a big balloon to go with it. I think that would be better than flowers anyway since it is a baby.'

The two flipped through a huge book of balloon possibilities and settled on a big one that was shaped like Noah's Ark. The colors were pastel, so they got some soft yellow, green, and white, smaller balloons to enhance the colors. 'Can you have this delivered to room 704 as soon as you have it ready? We are going to visit my daughter-in-law, and it would be nice for this to arrive while we are still in the room,' Judith suggested. "Give us about fifteen minutes and we will bring it up to her,' the attendant promised.

The nurse was just stepping out of the room when they arrived at Andrea's door. Josh was sitting by the window. He looked like he was ready to go to sleep. 'How are things going?' Judith asked as she gave Andrea a hug. 'The nurse just left and said that the doctor would be in this evening to see Andrea, and if everything goes as planned, they will probably release her first thing in the morning. We will not know until we talk to the doctor if he is going to put her on complete bed rest or not. We are hoping he will just tell her to take it easy, but we will do whatever we have to do,' Josh said with genuine concern. 'Have you eaten, Josh?' Sierra asked. 'Well, no, I thought about going to get something in a little bit, but I hate to leave Andrea here by herself,' he replied.

'Josh, I am going to take a nap anyway, go get yourself something to eat – and you can bring me something back. I think I have had all of the bland mashed potatoes I can take for one week,' she tried to laugh. 'Well it just so happens that Sierra and I were going to go eat after we left the hospital. Josh why don't you come? Go with us? We will drop you back off when you are done,' Judith invited him hoping he would agree. He needed to get out of that room for a bit and recuperate. 'Please Josh. Go with them. You need to get out of here for a while,' Andrea entreated. Josh agreed.

'Well, what's going on with the preacher guy, what's his name?' Andrea asked. 'His name is Grayson, and it is going really well,' Sierra answered. She didn't want to take the time to tell the whole story, especially since Andrea was still half lit on some sort of medication to keep her sedated. 'We had dinner last night at Pastor Allen's house, then we talked for a while, and he invited me to come to Tennessee with him next week for his cousin's wedding,' she summarized. 'Whoa, going to meet the family already, you don't waste any time do you sis,' Josh jested from the seat by the window. 'Ha! No, I guess not,' she said with a blush in her cheeks.

124

About that time there was a knock at the door. The lady from the gift shop came in with the elephant and balloons. 'That was fast,' Sierra thought. It looked perfect. 'Oh, who are those from,' Andrea said as she reached out for the card. When she saw that it was from Judith and Sierra she was very complimentary. 'That was so sweet guys, you didn't have to do that, but I love it!' she said in an effort to be gracious. 'Now ya'll go on and get some lunch. The quicker you go, the quicker I will get some good food in here too,' she laughed. 'What are you in the mood for,' Sierra asked. 'Anything but Chinese or Japanese,' Josh responded instead of Andrea, and in an adamant tone. 'What he said,' Andrea laughed. 'You know what I like Josh, I trust you. Have fun!'

Josh was tired, but much more relaxed than he had been the day before. He was relieved to know that things were going to be okay, and thankful they got to the hospital in time. 'I heard that new place over by the movie theater is supposed to be really good. It's some kind of cheesecake place, but they have everything you can imagine on the menu. Why don't we try that out,' he suggested. 'Why don't I just follow you over there so you don't have to come back to the hospital? There's no sense in backtracking,' he said thoughtfully. 'Okay, I know exactly where we are going, we will meet you there,' said Judith.

The cheesecake place quickly became Sierra's favorite restaurant. It was beautiful, the food was amazing, the servings were enormous, and the cheesecakes were so appealing that they each bought a piece to-go since they were too full to eat it in the restaurant. As they were asking for the check, they realized that they had forgotten to order something for Andrea. 'Oh, can we please see a menu. We need to place a to-go order if that would be possible. If you need us to we can wait in the lobby,' Josh said. 'By all means, stay where you are, I will refill your drinks. There is no rush,' she replied. 'I will order her the parmesan pasta with chicken, she will like that.' Josh said as he looked over the choices.

As they waited for Andrea's food, they discussed in more detail the relationship status of Grayson and Sierra. 'It sounds like I may have met your new brother-in-law,' Judith said to Josh. 'Well, mom, don't jump the gun. Things are going well, he did say that he too feels like there is something stirring between us, but we didn't go pick out rings or anything.' Sierra said bashfully. 'Well, we are going to look at wedding dresses after we eat Josh, so what does that tell you?' Judith announced. 'Now mom, you know that we were just going to do that for fun. There is nothing to it Josh, really, I do feel like he may be one I will marry someday, but I am not saying it is going to be tomorrow! I am not saying with certainty that it will ever be – but something is happening. That's all I know,' she made clear.

'You know you are going to have to bring him over so we can give you our approval before you make any kind of real decisions,' Josh poked in a fatherly tone. 'Well mom is the one who introduced me to him, so how is that for approval?' she said in reply to his remark.

It was not long before Andrea's food was ready and they headed out the door. 'Ya'll have fun playing dress-up and we will give you a call tomorrow evening when we get back home,' Josh said as he headed to his truck with a bag of food in his hand.

'Okay, it's about one-thirty in the afternoon now. Your dad gets home at about four thirty in the evening, so if we head home by about three thirty, that should give us plenty of time to go look at dresses and be home in time to get some supper on the stove. 'Sounds like a plan to me,' Sierra laughed ran to the car.

Sierra and Judith were both overwhelmed with the choices in the bridal store. Dress after dress, after dress was hanging on the racks and all she had to do was point to one and the attendant would put it in the dressing room. Just as Andrea told them, the attendant knew how to look at Sierra's height, weight, and other factors, and narrow down the choices that would work for her. She explained that any dress she tried on that did not fit correctly could be altered for free right there in the store after it was purchased.

Sierra was a bit sentimental standing in the bridal store with her mother. This was the day she had dreamt of since she was old enough to imagine what it would be like to be the one wearing a beautiful dress walking toward her prince charming. She could tell by the Judith's quiet demeanor that she too sensed the surreal ambiance of the moment, but she was careful to mention it in fear of making her cry.

Sierra picked full shirted gowns with flowing trains, fitted bodices, and flowing veils. Every dress that brought the image of a princess to her mind was sent away to the dressing room. 'I think we have a pretty good selection to start with if you want to go ahead and try them on, then if you are not pleased with any of them, we can go back to the drawing board. What do you say? The attendant encouraged. Sierra had a great time trying on the gowns, but it was difficult for Judith to get through the occasion without crying. She was happy and sad at the same time. 'Sierra, you look beautiful in every dress you put on, but of these, I like this one the best,' she said.

'Ok. Now that we have tried this style on, why don't we look at some dresses in a different style,' the attendant suggested. We have some gowns that are not as – well – for lack of a better word – fluffy, but they are extravagant and elegant. You may be surprised to find that you like them.

'You are a beautiful girl,' the lady went on with her sales pitch. 'You don't need so much dress to draw the attention of the audience and ultimately your groom. Your beauty will enhance the dress rather than the dress enhancing you. Does that make sense? And you can be sure I do not say that to everyone,' the attendant said, unrehearsed. Sierra laughed inside as that was her exact thought, 'she says that to everyone.'

She picked up one dress that looked almost like a silk scarf. Having had her mind on such full dresses, she thought there was not much to it, but she decided to try it on for kicks. As it turns out, it was the most beautiful dress she had tried on all day. It was as if it was made for her petite frame. Fitted from the neck to the knees, with a flowing bottom, laced with beads from the top to the bottom, Sierra barely recognized herself when she looked in the mirror. She looked back at her mother to see her wiping away the tears from her eyes.

'Okay, take it off Sierra – that's all I can take for one day,' Judith commanded. 'That's the one – but I can't look at you in it any more. Ma'am, if you would write down the information on that dress just in case we decide we want to get it one day I would really appreciate it,' Judith said as she rushed over to help Sierra get out of that dress. 'Boy, I wasn't expecting to feel what I just felt when I saw you in that dress,' she explained in a panic. This game of dress-up has got to be over because this momma can't take any more. One week has not been long enough for me to get prepared for this reality!'

Sierra got dressed while Judith went to the front to get the information on the dress. They left the bridal store and headed home.

Chapter Eighteen

When they got back to the house, Judith checked the answering machine. Sierra had received calls from both Travis and Grant. 'You need to call your brothers back. They both left you a message while we were gone. If I were you I would go ahead and call now while you are thinking about it,' she said.

Sierra called Grant first. 'Hey, I got your message, what's up?' she said as Grant answered his phone. 'Oh, Alisa wanted me to call and see if you had plans for tonight. She wanted to go to a movie or something. She's planning on having an early supper and then heading to the theater if you want to come,' he said. 'I actually don't have any plans for tonight. I was going to go by and see Presley, Rachael's baby, but I can always go by there on Monday. What time are you going to eat?' she inquired. 'Probably at around five-thirty, most of the movies start at around seven o'clock, so that will give us time to get there and get tickets beforehand,' he answered. 'Yeah, that sounds great. I will be there sometime after five o'clock. You need me to bring anything?' she asked. 'No, I think we just about have it all together. Just bring yourself,' he said cordially. 'Sounds like a plan, I will see you soon. Bye.'

Sierra hung up the phone and thought she would change out of those interview clothes before she called Travis. It had been a while since they had talked, so she knew it would be a long conversation. 'I think I will just wear my LSU sweats,' Sierra thought. 'I am just going to be with Grant and Alisa, who do I have to impress?' she thought as she gathered her sweat-suit and socks and headed to the bathroom. 'I think I might even just throw my cap on too. Why not? I have been dressed up all day long, I want to be comfortable.' She thought.

'Mom, I am going to call Travis. After that I am headed over to Grant and Alisa's house for dinner. I think we are going to see a movie too,' Sierra yelled through the door of Judith's bedroom. 'Okay honey, but if it gets too late, why don't you just stay over at their place tonight. I hate for you to be on the road by yourself that late,' Judith said sincerely. 'I'll see. Grayson is supposed to be here to pick me up at ten o'clock in the morning, so I would have to get up and come this way since I don't have a bag packed,' she said. 'Well why don't you go in there and pack yourself a bag real quick just to be on the safe side? That way if you decide to stay you won't have to worry about coming back to get ready, you can just get ready there,' she suggested. 'Okay – you're right – as usual. I will get a bag ready. We are just going to a carwash tomorrow, so I don't have to wear anything fancy,' she implied.

Sierra threw a few things in an overnight bag and went to the living room to call Travis. 'Hey stranger, how are you?' She said when he picked up on the other end of the line. "Boy, you are one hard fish to catch these days aren't you? Travis said with a laugh. 'You haven't been home but a little over a week and you've already burned the roads up,' he continued. 'I have been trying to call you every day and you are either gone, asleep, or gone,' he chided. 'Okay, okay – I get the point,' Sierra interjected. 'So, how have you been? I heard your base has been doing exercises this week. Are they over now?' she asked in an effort to change the subject.

'Yes, we finished up today. I am glad too. It is always more stressful during exercises on the base. You know how that is, everyone is ready to rest when they are over. So, how does it feel to be back in *La Maison*?' he asked. Well, I thought it was going to be a difficult transition after being away from here for so long, but as it turns out, God meant for me to be here, so it has been overwhelmingly perfect.

'Perfect; man, that's a pretty strong word what is going on?' 'I will not bore you with the long version, but I will tell you what is going on in a nutshell. I came home last week, mother asked me to go to church with her on Sunday to sing. She really wanted me to meet their Associate Pastor, but she arranged for me to sing so that it wouldn't be so obvious that I was there just to meet him. Well, to make a long story short, since the initial encounter with him my life has changed forever. I broke up with PJ on the day he called to finally say he loved me. I broke my cigarettes in half and threw them in the garbage when I heard God speak audibly to me in my car telling me to 'clean my glove box out.' I have no desire for the party life. I think he is the guy I am supposed to marry.

'Whoa! Wait a minute! The guy you are supposed to marry, what is wrong with you, Sierra, you can't know you are going to marry someone that you have not even known for a week. Snap out of it.' He said very directly. 'Well, until Sunday that is what I always thought too, but I am telling you this is different. God is all over it, and he is pulling me to Grayson like an electromagnet. Everyone who has been around us can feel it. Mom, Brother Allen, and Sabrina all are just as sure as I am that this is a God thing,' she explained in a desperate attempt to make him understand that she is not losing her mind.

His name is Grayson Raines. Dad calls him Grainey. I spent time with him in New Orleans with Rachael and Trish earlier in the week. They saw it too. If you could be here to meet him, I promise your doubt would fly away. Anyway, I went to church on Wednesday night after we got back from the hospital. Andrea is doing better, by the way. She is supposed to go home in the morning if everything goes as planned. She is probably just going to have to take it easy for the rest of the pregnancy.

Anyway, I went to dinner at the Pastor's house. Then after church I went back over to play games and stuff. We had a chance to talk and he invited me to go to Tennessee with him next week to his cousin's wedding. He wants me to meet his parents. Now that is a flip of the coin from PJ is it not!' she exclaimed.

'Yes, it is, but it is so fast. I worry about you getting yourself caught up in a relationship that you won't know how to get out of,' he explained. 'I am telling you; that has already happened. I am hooked, and I wasn't even trying. God did this, it is as if he played Cupid and shot me right in the heart, but the funny thing is, he shot Grayson too. I know it sounds ridiculous, but it is too real to deny,' she tried to explain but she could picture Travis sitting on the phone shaking his head at her.

'And, I got a job today,' she said. 'Well that's good, is it at the bank where you went yesterday?' 'Actually, they just called me yesterday. I went for the interview this morning in downtown Baton Rouge near the Capital building. It will start off as a temporary job. Then, if I impress them with my skills, they will hire me permanently with benefits, so I start in a week,' she filled him in on the details.

'I am going to Grant and Alisa's house tonight. We are going to eat and then go see a movie. I don't even know what's playing, but we will pick something out when we get there.' I wish you could go with us.' She told him. 'When will you get to come home?' she asked, knowing the answer would be different than what she wanted to hear. 'Well the truth is, before long. Don't tell mom yet, but I just got orders to Germany. I leave in about three months. I will get to come home for a week or so sometime between now and then, but I am not ready to tell mom and dad yet, so keep that under your hat. I want to make sure I have all of my ducks in a row before I get the twenty-one questions from Stan-the-Man. Right now I just have basic information, so I want to know more before I say anything,' he explained with nervous excitement.

'Oh man, Germany, I am going to hate you being that far away. That's like the very news I needed to end an almost perfect week,' she said sarcastically. 'Oh, now don't feel that way. I am excited about it. One of the reasons I wanted to be in the Air Force to begin with was to see the world. This will be my first real chance to do that. Be happy for me!' he exacted.

'I am. I am happy for you, just not so happy for me,' she admitted with a saddened heart. 'I promise I won't say anything to mom and dad. Is it okay if I tell Alisa and Grant tonight while I am with them?' she asked. He answered with hesitancy, but said if they promised to keep it between us until he was ready to let mom and dad know, that would be fine. 'I am sure that won't be a problem. Thank you for telling me, even though it isn't exactly what I wanted to hear!' she reverberated.

'Well, it is getting close to five o'clock and Alisa said they wanted to eat an early dinner at around five-thirty. I had better get going or I am going to be late. It was really nice to talk to you. I will keep you posted on the whole Grayson thing, and I will keep all of that other stuff under my hat!' she said. 'Ok, well it was good to talk to you too,' he said. 'I love you,' she concluded.

'I love you too,' he said as he hung up the phone. 'Okay mom and dad, I am going to go to Grant's now. I guess I will plan to stay there with them tonight so I don't have to drive late at night and worry you. I will be back before Grayson gets here in the morning. I love you,' she said as she grabbed her bag and scurried out the door.

Chapter Nineteen

'Proverbs 16: 9: A man's mind plans his way, but the Lord directs his steps and makes them sure, Proverbs 16: 9.' Sierra pondered the words of that verse in her heart as she approached Grant and Alisa's driveway. 'Thank you Lord for arresting me and making sure I did not go the wrong way. If I never believed your Words before, I do now. I can't deny the truth in the Words you spoke because I suddenly see them coming to light in my life before my very eyes.' Sierra prayed.

She felt almost like God had reached down into a world full of people and picked her for his miracle work. 'What did I do to deserve to be chosen God?' she asked out loud as she parked her car and sat in the driveway in silence. 'Your word says that if we delight ourselves in you – then you will give us the desire of our heart. God – you know I was not delighting myself in you, yet you have given me the desire of my heart anyway – and I didn't even know it was there!

Help me to walk in your way. Help me to be what you are calling me to be, because Lord –I don't know how. All I know is that you instantly changed me from the inside out. You have blessed me with the possibility of a future far different from anything I could have ever imagined, or hoped for, and you have placed a man in my life that I could never have found in my own futile search. I feel humbled and blessed, but I am scared at the same time. I know in my own strength I will mess everything up. I need you to be my strength

God. I need you to finish this work that you have started in me.'
She petitioned.

Sierra inhaled deeply and let it out to the count of five before
going inside. 'Hey guys,' she said as she peeked through the front
door. 'Hey – Sierra, come on in,' Grant said as he walked toward the
table with a hot dish in his hands. 'You are just in time – the chicken
casserole just came out of the oven. Alisa is in the kitchen getting the
drinks. Go tell her what you want,' he directed. Alisa gave Sierra a
welcoming hug as she entered the kitchen. 'I poured you sweet tea.
Is that alright?' Alisa asked. 'With no lemon, you know me. Thanks
Alisa.' She replied.

Over dinner Sierra brought Grant and Alisa up-to-date. 'Boy, it
seems like it has been a year since we talked. So much has happened
in the past few days that I don't even know where to start,' she
divulged. 'I went to New Orleans with Rachael and Trish on
Tuesday. Mom arranged for Pastor Allen to call Grayson and tell
him we were going to be there just in case he wanted to try to catch
up with us. Well – he did. He showed up at the fountain on the
River Walk and we got some beignets. Rachael and Trish asked him
a bunch of questions and he answered them all. You won't believe
this, but he almost went to the Olympics,' she boasted.

That tidbit of information captured Grant's interest above
everything else. 'Wait, did you say the Olympics? What was he
going to compete in and why *almost*?' he asked inquisitively. Sierra
explained to Grant that Grayson was a power lifter. She gave him
the whole spill about Mr. Tennessee and the incident at the National
Championships that gave Grayson fourth place rather than the
title. She then explained that God told Grayson he was finished
competing and he had a choice to make. She told them about the
sponsorships with huge corporations and all of the fame and fortune
that was right at his fingertips. 'God gave Grayson a choice,' she
explained. He basically told him that he could go his own way, or
he could walk in the way that God had for him. 'This is the way,
walk ye in it,' she quoted.

He chose to give all of that up and follow God. That's why he is at the seminary and working at *Flowing Creek Church* rather than living in San Francisco training for the Olympics.

'Wow, that's quite a story,' Grant answered in astonishment. 'So, anyway, he told us a lot about himself. The next day I went over to the Allen's house for dinner before the Wednesday night services. Grayson and I talked for long time after church that night. He focused on me and asked questions in an effort to get to know me better. He said that it was obvious there was something going on between us and he was not in a position to run from God again. He asked me if he could have a picture of me because he wanted to show it to his friends at the seminary. Then, he invited me to go to his cousin's wedding with him next week in Tennessee. He wants his parents to meet me,' Sierra looked to Alisa for reassurance.

'Well, you don't waste time – do you,' Grant said with a grin. 'No – really, it sounds like it is truly God doing a work in your life and I am really happy for you. So, when can we meet this guy?' Grant said with authority. 'Well – he is picking me up tomorrow morning at mom and dad's house to go to a carwash. I don't know, why don't you guys come to *Flowing Creek Church* on Sunday morning, I know he will be there,' she said with a chuckle. 'We may just do that,' Grant said as he looked over at Alisa and nodded. 'I am so excited! I love it when a plan comes together,' Alisa said as she clapped her hands enthusiastically.

'Thanks for inviting me to come over tonight. You don't know it yet, but I am not going back to mom and dad's house after the movie. I am going to be the houseguest, who never goes away,' she laughed. 'Now – Sierra, you know you are welcome to stay here any time, for as long as you want to,' Grand insisted. 'Thanks! I appreciate that. Mom doesn't like to sit up and worry about me when I am out late. It will calm her nerves to know I am not driving all the way back out there tonight,' she said knowing Grand and Alisa knew full well how Judith felt.

'Oh, and speaking of mom's nerves, I have something to tell you guys that can't go past this table,' she revealed. 'What? I love secrets,' Alisa responded. 'I talked to Travis today. He got orders to Germany.' 'Oh my goodness, mom is going to croak. When is he leaving?' Grant asked with a worried look on his face. 'He has to finish up some project he is in the middle of in New Mexico, then he has a few training classes he has to go through before he flies out. He said it would be two or three months. He doesn't have all of the details ironed out just yet. That is the reason he isn't ready for mom and dad to find out. He said he wants to be well prepared for the game of twenty questions Stan-the-man is going to throw at him. They all laughed. 'You've gotta love Mr. Stan,' Alisa said with a smile.

'Well girls, we had better get a move on if we are going to get to the theater before all of the good movies start. I don't even know what's playing, so it will be good to get there a few minutes early to read up on our choices. 'Yeah, I will agree, we had better go. Let's just put these dishes in the sink and we can get to them when we get back,' Alisa suggested.

Sierra enjoyed the evening with Grant and Alisa. They were always so understanding and supportive. Sierra could relax and be herself around them. She liked that. After the movie, they finished the dishes, then sat around and played a word game until it was time to go to bed. It was the most unstressed evening Sierra had all week, and she told them that.

The next morning Sierra woke up, took a shower, got dressed, gathered up her things, and was ready to go. 'Thanks again guys!' She said as she headed toward the door. 'The dinner was great – and I really enjoyed hanging out with you. Remember, 'mums the word' on Travis.'

'Okay, Sierra – thanks for coming! We enjoyed it. Our lips are sealed!' Grant shouted from the living room. Sierra wanted to get to her parent's house early enough to be there when Grayson arrived to pick her up for the carwash.

To her surprise, she saw Grayson's car sitting in her parent's driveway when she pulled in. Looking at the clock on her dashboard she realized that it was only a few minutes past nine. 'Grayson said he would be there at ten,' she wondered why he had come early. One thing was certain, she was very glad she decided to get ready at Grant's house before she went home. She would have hated to walk in the door looking like she just woke up.

'Hey' – she said as she walked in the door and saw Grayson sitting at the table with Stan in front of a huge platter of pancakes. 'I called last night and your mom told me you weren't home. When I told her I would be by at ten to pick you up, she insisted I come at nine for some pancakes with Stan. I couldn't resist the offer,' Grayson said as he heaped his plate with pancakes. 'Come eat with us,' her dad said as he almost emptied the syrup bottle onto his plate.

'No thanks, dad, I am not really into breakfast. I would rather wait and eat a good lunch later on,' she said as she pulled up a chair. 'What time did you get here Grayson?' she asked. 'Actually; I had not been here very long when you came in,' he said. Stan went on to question Grayson about how many cars they hoped to wash, how much money they were trying to raise, and how long they were going to work before calling it quits. 'We have about fifteen-hundred dollars left to raise before we go to camp this summer, I hope to knock a decent sized chunk off of that total,' he said hopefully. 'We will start at ten-thirty, and we will wash cars until they quit coming or until we run out of soap, whichever happens first.'

'Well, have fun,' Stan said. 'I am sure glad God didn't call me to be a preacher. I would not want to do the things that you guys have to do,' he joked. 'Stan, the world is also glad that God didn't call you to be a preacher,' Judith said as she laughed aloud at the thought.

Grayson and Sierra went to the church to meet the youth group at a few minutes before ten. They loaded the youth into the church van and headed to the mall parking lot where Grayson had permission to set up and wash cars. Throughout the course of the day, the group retaliated on Sierra repeatedly for her resistance to the water hose last Sunday night. She was like a wet noodle by the end of the day.

'Ha! Ha! I love it, Grayson cackled as he threw her a towel. 'One-hundred cars at three dollars a pop – plus whatever we got in the donation box. That should just about wind it up,' he said.

Sierra enjoyed the day. There was no pressure to perform and no awkward 'alone' moments. The teenagers jeered all day long making remarks about Grayson flirting, or Sierra trying to impress him, but they were not bothered by them. 'It is what it is,' there is no since in acting like we aren't drawn to each other,' she thought.

After cleaning and loading the van, Grayson headed back to the church to drop the youth off. Most of them had a car, but Grayson and Sierra had to wait a few minutes for others to call for a ride. Pastor Allen drove up while they waited for the parents of the last two youth.

'What are ya'll doing tonight?' he said to Grayson and Sierra. 'I don't know yet. We just got back – the first thing we need to do is get out of these wet clothes. Why, what did you have in mind?' Grayson asked. 'Sabrina and I are taking the boys to that big buffet they just opened in Baton Rouge over on the old highway, ya'll are welcome to join us if you would like to.'

Grayson looked over at Sierra. He knew she had to be hungry since she didn't eat breakfast and they had not stopped washing cars to get lunch. 'What do you think?' he said. 'That's fine with me,' she replied timidly. About that time a car pulled into the driveway. 'I'll take both of those stragglers,' Ted Roberts said as he hung his head out of the window of his truck. The last two teenagers climbed into the back of Ted's truck and waved as he drove away.

'I will run Sierra home so she can get ready. It's about four-thirty now. What time do you want to leave?' Grayson asked Pastor Allen. 'Well, Sabrina won't be back until at least five, why don't we shoot for six o'clock. 'Okay, that sounds good,' he agreed.

'Come on Sierra, hop in my car and I will take you home. He waited until they were in the car and said, 'I really appreciate you for coming with me today. I was afraid I might have scared you off after our little talk Wednesday night,' he said as he patted her on the knee.

'Well, Grayson Raines, if you were trying to scare me off, your plans failed miserably. All I can think about is the next time I will get to see you,' she acknowledged. 'I am so excited about going to Tennessee with you,' she said. Sierra told Grayson about her new job, and the fact that it would not begin until after the trip, so she was free to go. He was visibly thrilled. 'I am so glad. That will give us the trip up there to talk and get to know each other better,' he said as if he had already given that some thought beforehand. 'I was going to leave out Monday morning very early, but since you are going to go, I may ask Pastor Allen if we can head out tomorrow afternoon after church is over. That way we won't be in such a rush,' his mind was running with ideas as he pulled in the Bradley's driveway. 'What should I pack for the trip?' Sierra asked sincerely. 'Well, the wedding is Friday night, so you will need to bring something nice to wear for that, but other than that – you can just bring whatever you want to wear. Believe me, you won't have to worry about impressing anybody,' he assured her.

'Okay – I will see you after a while then. Are you going to drive, or will we ride with the Allen's?' she asked. Grayson winked at her just as the sun caught his left eye. It sparkled at the very moment he said, 'I will drive; I don't want to share you with the Allen boys.' Sierra blushed, closed his door, and went on inside to get ready to go again.

'Hey mom,' she said as she walked in the door. 'Hey! How did it go?' Judith asked. 'We raised three hundred dollars from washing the cars, then whatever is in the donation box, we didn't count that yet,' she said. 'Well great – maybe just a few more and they will reach their goal,' she said encouragingly.

'Pastor Allen invited Grayson and me to go out to eat with his family tonight. Grayson is going to pick me up at around six. If Pastor Allen agrees, I think we are going to head to Tennessee after tomorrow morning's service. Oh – by the way, I invited Grant and

Alisa to come. They want to meet Grayson, and I thought that would be the best way,' she said.

'That will be good. Josh is going to be there too. Andrea finally went home from the hospital this morning. She is not on complete bed-rest, but almost. The doctor wants her to do as little as possible. So, if she is up to it she will come too. If not, Josh will bring her here while we go to church and they will stay for lunch afterwards. That's why I am making cookies. I was trying to get ahead of the game. Will you and Grayson be able to eat with us before you head out?' she asked. 'I would think so, but we will not stay long afterwards. It is about a ten-hour drive to his parent's house, so we don't want to be driving all night long,' she said.

'Okay, that will be fine. I am glad everyone is going to get a chance to meet him. I know they will love him.' Judith said with confidence. 'I sure hope so,' Sierra said. 'I enjoyed spending time with him today in a carefree environment. We were just able to be ourselves. The kids were picking at us all day long, and he never denied a thing. I think Grayson was enjoying the moment, making them speculate whether their assumptions about us were correct. 'All I know is that I was enjoying watching him run around in that cut-off, soaking wet, t-shirt all day long. I think at least half of the cars we washed were there because the girls driving them wanted to get a closer look at him,' she laughed. 'Hey it works with pretty girls, why not Mr. America in a cut-off shirt,' she laughed.

Sierra and Grayson met the Allen's at the restaurant. As it turned out, it was a Mexican, all-you-can-eat buffet. Grayson loved that, he ate more chicken enchiladas than the pan could hold. 'A big boy with a big appetite,' Pastor Allen said. 'That's why we try to find buffets. When we agreed to feed him on the weekends as part of his pay package, we didn't know what we were getting ourselves into,' he sniggered. Grayson just laughed.

After the meal the Pastor and his family were going bowling. Grayson and Sierra decided not to go with them because they still had to pack and get ready for their trip the following day.

'You can hang out at my mom and dad's house with me for a while if you want to,' Sierra invited. You can talk to me while I get my suitcase packed. 'That sounds like a plan,' he said as they walked to his car. By this time the sun had gone down and full moon was shining overhead.

When they were almost halfway to the Bradley's house, Grayson pulled the car over in a church parking lot. He cut off the engine, and turned on the interior light. Sierra wondered what he was going to do. For a long time he sat with his eyes turned toward her. 'Just let me look at you. Please, don't say a word,' he implored. Sierra felt almost weird sitting in complete silence with Grayson just staring at her. She tried to make eye contact with him a time or two, but he did not waver, she wasn't even sure he ever blinked his eyes. After waiting long enough that she felt uncomfortable, she said, 'What are you looking at?' Then finally he responded.

'I think I am looking at the girl I am in love with.' Sierra thought she would faint. Her head began spinning, and her heart was pounding so hard that she could feel it in her ears. 'I showed your picture to everyone I came in contact with at the seminary. I told them they needed to see what God was capable of doing when we are willing to wait on him and follow his leading. 'I am not totally sure that you feel the same way, but I have to be honest with you before we go to Tennessee. I think you are the girl I am supposed to spend the rest of my life with. I think you are going to be my wife.'

Sierra felt a tear roll down her cheek and Grayson's tender hand reach over to wipe it off. As he did, be tilted her chin towards him; giving Sierra no choice but to look into his amazing eyes as he continued. 'I am going to do something right now that I have never done in my life,' he said. 'I am going to make a commitment to you. I don't know what God has in store for our future, but until I find out, I will not date another person. I give you a promise that you have my undivided attention as we walk along this path that God has obviously laid out for us. I will be open and honest with you, so if there is anything you want to know, just ask. I would like to ask the same from you, but I will not push you. I know that this is really happening fast, believe me I feel like my head is spinning, but I know what God is telling me, and I have to obey,' as he finished his sentence, he let go of her chin and took her hand.

Sierra was overwhelmed, but she felt exactly the same way. Every word Grayson spoke paralleled her own feelings and thoughts. Every nerve in her body felt a shiver, she welcomed the warmth of is hand in hers. 'Well, I was not expecting this to come from you, at least not yet, but there is no denying what is real,' Sierra said. 'I am drawn to you like a magnet and I can't imagine ever wanting to pursue another relationship. I will make a commitment you as well. Until we know what God is doing here, I will focus on what He wants for this relationship. I don't have any problem making that promise. Right now I think it will be one of the easiest promises to keep that I have ever made,' she said with a little smile.

'Can I kiss you?' Grayson asked nervously. He said that he didn't want to mess things up. He didn't want to move too fast. But he could not resist asking for just a small kiss on her lips to seal their agreement. 'Sierra knew this moment was going to come. She had nervously anticipated it since the first time she laid her eyes on Grayson. She thought to herself, 'of course you can kiss me.'

Grayson reached across the seats and placed his warm hands against Sierra's cheeks and pulled her close to him. As his tender lips met hers, she felt the same electrifying shock go through her body that she felt the first time he touched her when she walked into the fellowship hall that first morning after they met. It was as if he froze in that spot the moment his lips touched hers, and he didn't ever want to let go. 'A still, innocent kiss to seal their commitment, this guy is too much,' she thought as she enjoyed the moment. Grayson tenderly pulled away, but only far enough to look directly into Sierra's eyes, 'Thank you!' he said, 'Thank you for allowing God to direct your steps.'

With that, Grayson turned off the interior light and drove Sierra home. He reached over and put his hand on top of hers as they pulled into her parent's driveway. 'I am honored that you will go with me to Tennessee tomorrow. I wouldn't have wanted to go without you.'

Grayson parked the car, they got out and headed to the front door, but on the way there Grayson stopped Sierra. He wrapped his arms around her and hugged her with the most affectionate hug she had ever received in her life. She wanted to melt into his arms. She was blessed.

Chapter Twenty

Grayson sat in the living room visiting with Stan. Sierra brought her clothes and suitcase in and sat on the floor packing them up while they talked. Stan gave Grayson the 'daddy' treatment. Sierra expected it, but she knew Grayson was a little bit nervous as he guarded his answers with every bit of discretion he could muster. 'When did you graduate from college, what other jobs did you have before you decided to become a preacher, why did you quit competing, why didn't you at least let a few of those sponsors take you on for just a little while, son, you could have had more money than you would have known what to do with if you would have done that, and are you sure you want this squirrely little thing to go to Tennessee with you, she is liable to go off in those hills and get lost,' he went on and on.

Sierra just smiled at Grayson and shook her head. 'He might as well get used to it if things are going to go as they were thinking, this would be his life story,' she thought. Sierra went and got the new dress she bought with her mom earlier in the week to show it to Grayson. 'Do you think this will be okay to wear to your cousin's wedding?' she asked. 'Perfect,' he said as he winked, clicked his tongue, and gave her a thumb's up. 'I don't want to cram it into the suitcase or it will get wrinkled. I was going to wear it to church tomorrow morning, but I think I will wait and wear it to the wedding so it will not get dirty. 'I have a hanging bag that I am going to put in my car with my suit in it, if you want I will take it and put it in there too,' he suggested.

'I will just go ahead and take this because I have to pack my things before I call it a night too. Sierra if you want to leave your suitcase here once you have it packed, we can swing by here on our way out and pick it up. 'Well, mom had planned on us staying long enough to eat lunch before we left anyway, so that will work out fine.

Sierra walked Grayson to the door and gave him one last hug. She felt him kiss the top of her head before he walked away. 'I will just throw a sweat suit in the car and change here before we go tomorrow if that's okay. 'That will be great! See you in the morning, goodnight!'

Sierra went directly into the bathroom and closed the door. She needed to catch her breath and process everything that had just taken place. She was not ready to answer Judith and Stan's questions just yet. She looked in the mirror and said, 'Is this really happening.' She felt like she was in the middle of a dream that he hoped would never end.

Sierra finished packing her suitcase; then she got her clothes ready for Sunday morning's service. 'I think I am going to go on to bed. Tomorrow is going to be a long day,' she said. About that time Judith walked in, 'I am sorry I was not able to come visit with Grayson while he was here,' she explained. 'I was on the phone with my sister, they are going through some difficult times with their daughter right now and she needed a shoulder to cry on.' 'Is everything going to be okay?' Sierra asked. 'Yes, I think so. It is just some of those issues that every family has to face. She will be fine, but I needed to be there for her tonight, that's all,' she answered. 'Well I know she was glad you were. I know if I am going through something I sure do feel good to know that you are there for me.' Sierra confessed.

'You are sweet, goodnight honey,' she said.

Sierra slept like a baby. When the alarm clock sounded for her to get ready for church the following morning, she was actually rested. It was one of few days Sierra could remember not wanting to turn over and go back to sleep. She wasn't sure if it was due to the excitement of the trip with Grayson, or because she had gone to bed early. It was probably a combination of the two, but more than anything else it was excitement. 'It's like when you know you have a plane to catch at dark-thirty in the morning and you are wide awake an hour before the alarm clock goes off,' she thought. At any rate, she got up, got ready for church, finished packing her suitcase, and was ready to go. She found herself pacing the floor, watching the clock, and anxious as it was too early for her to go to the church just yet. There would be no one there. Judith was usually one of the first ones there and she was not even ready to go yet. Hmmm, Sierra sighed as she felt her nerves begin to knot up in her stomach, let me see if there is anything I can watch on television while I am waiting to get my mind off of things, I have such nervous energy, she thought to herself.

She sat in the recliner and turned on the television. Flipping through the channels, she came across a documentary about the treasures and kings of Egypt. She found that quite interesting and it calmed her nerves while she waited on Judith and Stan to say they were ready to go. By the time they finally were ready, Sierra hated to turn it off, she found herself caught up in the treasures. 'I guess my 'turn the television on to calm your nerves' trick worked,' she laughed as she rustled around to find the remote so she could turn it off.

'I guess I will just ride with you since we are all going to the same place,' she said. 'Okay then, let's go,' Stan said as he grabbed the keys to his truck.

Sierra was anxious for Alisa, Grant, Josh and Andrea to meet Grayson. She hoped they would show up for church. As she entered the sanctuary with her parents, Pastor Allen was standing by the door pointing his finger behind him. 'He's in the back, we all know who you are looking for,' he said. Sierra was embarrassed just a little because all of the senior adults were sitting in the pews waiting for their Sunday school class to begin and heard that remark. About that time Laura Trahan, the red-head, walked up behind her and said sarcastically, 'Yeah, Sierra, we all know who you are looking for.' Sierra just rolled her eyes over to her mom and said, 'What is her problem?' 'I'll tell you in a minute,' she whispered as they walked toward the organ.

When Laura was out of sight, Judith explained to her that ever since Grayson came in view of a call to *Flowing Creek Church*, Laura had been almost stalking him. She had cornered him on several occasions and asked him to go to their house for dinner, and other things. He never gave her the time of day, so when you showed up and Grayson was showing you attention, Laura got jealous. She knows now that there is something between you two and she just wishes it was her. 'Ignore her,' she said. 'I have been ignoring her stuff since I was five years old, I should be a pro at it by now,' they both laughed and went their separate ways.

Alisa and Grant showed up just as the service was about to begin. Sierra had a quick chance to introduce them to Grayson, but only long enough for a handshake and a simple greeting. They sat down, once again on the front pew, for convenience, and Sierra turned to make eye contact with Alisa, who was sitting on the pew directly behind her. She recognized her facial expressions to be in complete approval of the choice God had made for her. 'He is really good looking,' she whispered, but loudly enough that Sierra was afraid everyone around them heard her, including Grayson. She looked up at him and he was grinning. 'She thinks I'm cute, huh,' he whispered. Sierra felt her stomach hit her feet, she thought she would die. But instead, she looked at him and said, 'yeah, and so do I.'

At the end of the service, Grayson and Sierra did not wait around to shake hands with the crowd. They slipped out the back door and went as quickly as they could to the Bradley's house. When they arrived, Andrea and Josh were sitting at the kitchen table waiting for everyone to get home. 'Hey, you made it!' Sierra said as she noticed they were there. 'I have someone I would like for you guys to meet.

This is Grayson Raines. He is the youth minister at *Flowing Creek Church*. Grayson, this is my brother Josh, and his wife Andrea. She is expecting their first baby.' Sierra said. As Grayson reached over to shake Josh's hand he said, 'I have been praying for you and your wife this week. I am glad to hear everything is going to be okay.' 'Thank you very much, I appreciate that,' Josh said with sincerity.

'Sierra, where would be the best place for me to go change out of this suit?' he said. 'Just go right in that bedroom by the front door if you want to. No one will bother you in there. I will go change too and then I will bring my suitcase out so we can load it into your car and get that over with.

By the time Grayson and Sierra were changed and ready to load the car, Alisa and Grant were in the kitchen and Judith and Stan were already changing their clothes too. 'I didn't get a chance to talk to you much at the church Grayson, but I am glad to meet you,' Grant said when he walked into the room. Everyone made him feel welcome and Sierra was glad. Andrea was prodding Sierra behind her back, whispering, 'you go girl,' in her ear, causing Sierra's cheeks to turn as red as fire.

Judith came in and took charge. "Now listen everybody, these two have a long way to drive today, so they need to get on the road. They need to get in here right now and fix their plates first. Ya'll go ahead and eat and don't wait for us – we don't want you to have to be getting there any later than you have to,' she said as she shoved a couple of plates in their hands. 'When you come to the Bradley house Grayson, you are going to be treated like family – so get over there and fix your own plate!' She chuckled as she tried to make him feel welcome. 'Yes ma'am. I believe I will,' he said as he moved toward the stove area where the post were lined up and filled with food.

He was still not used to Cajun food, so he was not sure what to do with the rice. Sierra laughed at him as she told him to get some rice on his plate then put the meat and gravy over it. 'In Tennessee we usually just eat potatoes,' he admitted, I guess I have a lot to learn.

They ate quickly, and were on their way. Sierra was anxious about the long trip with just the two of them. What would they talk about for that long? Where would they stop to eat? What if the car broke down, and a million other questions flooded her mind.

As Grayson's tries approached the end of the gravel driveway, he stopped the car. He looked at Sierra and said, 'Be anxious for nothing, but in everything through prayer and supplication, let your requests be made known unto God,' So, God, we pray today before we drive another inch of this journey - that you will watch over us. Protect us Lord as we are on the road. Let us make good time, not have any trouble with our vehicle, and not get any tickets or accidents. Show us the places where we need to stop along the way, whether it is to eat, or to get gas. We are trusting in you Lord. We give this trip to you. Put your angels around the front and the back of this car as we drive. We love you. Amen.'

Sierra had never even thought of praying like that before a trip. She was amazed at the calm that came over her as soon as he began to pray. *This is not our trip. This is God's trip and I have nothing to fear.* Sierra was learning so much about what it means to walk in the path that God lays out rather than her own. She wondered what lessons were waiting for her this week in Tennessee.

CPSIA information can be obtained at www.ICGtesting.com
Printed in the USA
BVOW08s1029190416

444756BV00001B/26/P